satisfy my soul

ALSO BY COLIN CHANNER

Waiting in Vain

Got to Be Real (a collection of four novellas)

A NOVEL

satisfy my soul

COLIN CHANNER

ONE WORLD

BALLANTINE BOOKS • NEW YORK

A One World Book
Published by The Ballantine Publishing Group

www.ballantinebooks.com/one/

Library of Congress Cataloging-in-Publication Data is available upon request from
the publisher.

ISBN 0-345-43789-6

Manufactured in the United States of America

First Edition: February 2002

10 9 8 7 6 5 4 3 2 1

For Kwame Dawes, my refuge and
faith healer.

*"And Jacob served seven years for Rachel;
and they seemed unto him* but *a few
days, for the love he had to her."*

GENESIS 29:20

*"Thou shalt not bow down thyself to them, nor serve them:
for I the Lord thy God* am *a jealous God, visiting the
iniquity of the fathers upon the children unto the
third and fourth* generation of them that hate me."

EXODUS 20:5

satisfy my soul

● CHAPTER ONE

Up ahead a herd of cattle toddles down a path. They moo and jostle as they splash into the ocher river, triggering the flowers on a tree festooned with Spanish moss to burst into a spray of screeching birds.

In theory this is stunning. But in Jamaica, an island that produces elemental drama daily, no one stops to look. Not the women spreading clothes on white boulders. Not the naked children swinging out on leafy vines. Not the men in trunks and soccer shorts who wade upstream, waist deep, empty bamboo rafts in tow, hunched against the current, delivering the vessels to the starting point for tips.

Fifteen feet away from us the captain of our raft is punting with a slender pole. The braided muscles in his back are coiling. His navy polo shirt is snug. Water tongues the grooves between the knuckled stems that form the hull. In essence we are sailing on a fence.

People are watching me. Waiting. A bead of perspiration stretches from my beard and bursts against my shirt.

Then as the captain steers around a bar of silt I find a question.

"Okay, Chadwick, on the night before you're set to go to the gallows you get a set of choices. A last book. A last song. A last meal with any writer living or dead. And the chance to sleep with anyone in the whole wide world—a *living* anyone, of course."

The producer on the raft beside us smiles and makes a fist. This is how she told me that she wants the show to be—arch and energetic.

I am a guest on *Trapped in Transit*, a travel show on A&E.

Each week on *TIT*, as all the members of the crew appear to call it, an odd couple chosen from the worlds of politics and entertainment take a journey: Howard Stern and Yasir Arafat canoeing in Mongolia. Martha Stewart and Biz Markie on a llama in Peru.

Chadwick is a congressman. If his reparations bill is passed, every black American will receive a million dollars in exchange for relocation to Liberia.

I'm a playwright and director whose grandfather moved to Harlem from West Africa in the twenties.

Chadwick is fifty. I am thirty-eight. Chadwick is married. I will never be. He is a Republican. I like to call myself a negro. He is bald. My locks are wrapped around my head to form a turban.

His freckled cheeks are settling into jowls. His nose is sharp and owlish. He does not have an upper lip. His forehead lasts forever.

"I think I'd have a rack of lamb," he answers. "And it is always hard for me to sleep without my wife. My favorite book has always been *Heart of Darkness*. Conrad is amazing. You should read him. I would dine with Rudy Kipling. As a boy in Oklahoma I felt connected to his stories . . . all the Indians. I know that our natives aren't the same as Kipling's Hindus, but I could still relate. As far as music is concerned I think I'd listen to Aretha Franklin. And you—you asked the question. What would you do?"

I glance at the producer, a desert-colored woman with a secret trail of bites along her neck and stomach. Her name is Amaranta.

Smiling as she looks away, she scoops her copper hair into a ponytail. When she looks again I recognize the contour of her body in her nose. Like her back, it arches inward on a bony spine then flares into a bulb of spongy flesh.

The diamonds on her wedding ring are glinting. Her cheeks are hard and chiseled like the stones. But as a woman she is soft. Her skin. Her voice. Her touch.

Last night, as she read to me in bed, I told her that her skin reminded me of sand. She drew her nipple on my chest and said I was her Tuareg . . . the way I wrap my dreadlocks like a turban, the oily blackness of my skin, the height of what she calls my Libyan nose. She held me by my cheekbones when she kissed me. She christened them my little horns.

"Ride all over me," she whispered. "Find water."

Chadwick leans toward me.

"On my final night on earth I would experiment with pork."

"You would cook it in a whole new way?"

"More than that. I've never had it. My father was a member of the Nation of Islam. My mother is a Jew."

"So you're mixed," he says appraisingly. His voice is engaged but impersonal, as if I were a piece of art. "I would not have known."

"And now you do. What does that mean?"

"Well . . . nothing."

"So why did you ask? What does it mean in terms of reparations? Do I get less for being a diluted brother or do I get a little extra for the Holocaust?"

"And what would be your book?" he asks me after we have sailed a mile in silence.

"I would read the Book of Psalms. I'd listen to "Redemption

Song" and eat some fish and bread with my closest friend Kwabena Small, the best playwright I know."

"And what would be the other choice? The woman?"

I burrow through the crates that line the basement of my mind and mount a retrospective of my lovers. It's an exhibit of ambitious scope. The catalog is thicker than a phone book. I can't decide. But I know that I have loved them all . . . at some time . . . in some way . . . with some degree of faithfulness and truth.

We argue politics until we disembark at Rafter's Rest, a restaurant and bar that occupies what used to be a rambling house: white walls, soft arches, slim columns.

Just beyond the restaurant the river broadens as it sweeps into the sea.

A buffet lunch is laid out on the covered esplanade: jerk chicken, curried conch, pasta salad, and escoveitched fish . . . fried snappers marinated in a habanero vinaigrette.

On the opposing bank, old trees with silver trunks and thick uplifted roots like rocket fins are soaring to the sky.

I sit alone. I cannot eat. My mind is exhausted. I keep returning to the question. Who would the woman be?

I go outside to think inside the minivan. If I had driven on my own I would leave.

The Isuzu is parked in a ring of vans beneath a poinciana tree aflame with red blossoms. The drivers are clotted in ragged groups, playing cards, chewing cane and smoking—from the odor, more than cigarettes.

Resurfacing the driveway is a gang of men who've clearly learnt the art of pouring asphalt by telepathy.

Everything is slow, and then a whistle rifles from the road. Suddenly everything is frantic. Men begin to dig and mix and roll and cart, while splashing their bodies with beer, brewing perspiration.

A mud-encrusted pickup trundles through the gate. It stops

abruptly and a female voice demands a work report. From the driver's side a bangled hand slides through the open window. The hand unrolls a fist and fans the foreman forward. He dips his head inside the cab. There is a sharp exchange and then he straightens up, a little softer in his posture, and watches as the Ford begins to roll toward me, the driver searching for a radius of shade.

As she walks toward the restaurant, the woman with the bangles stops and reaches in a tote bag for a telephone. She is tall, with dreadlocks braided in a fat chignon. She is calling someone whom she knows quite well, for she dials without looking.

"Don't fret, I'll soon be there," she says with a mischievously guilty laugh.

"But there is no story," she emphasizes. "Same story. Didn't I tell you that I don't want no lover till the right one comes? Anyway. I have to go and brutalize these lazy men that work for me." She begins to walk, then stops again. "Mind your business. There is no story to tell, I said. A lover would only distract me now."

That night I meet *my* lover at a lodge up in the mountains. I am staying at a hotel on the beach.

"Sleeping in your bed last night was absolutely careless," Amaranta mutters as she cracks the door. "And all these marks you left on me. What am I going to tell my husband?"

The room is long and narrow. At the other end, beyond the double bed, the drapes are flung apart. Through the sliding door come mist and chill and insect sounds, the smell of grass and pine.

A kerosene lamp is seeping amber light into the grooves between the planks that form the wooden walls. We are standing by the dresser. I hold her from behind, resting my chin on her head.

Her short nightgown is blue. She smells of ginger oil and citrus . . . maybe tangerine.

Watching our reflection in the mirror, I reach beneath her nightgown and my fingers find the ripples in her stomach. As the hem begins to flounce I see the creamy smoothness of her thighs, the hint of twitching muscle, the mole below the crescent of her bikini wax; there, the skin is dusky rose and prickly.

As I stroke her there she arcs her back and smiles, then sucks her teeth and shuts her eyes and presses all her softness into me.

I reach below her stomach for the scar she earned while bearing children. There is a lip of fat on either side. I pinch it and she moans. As I kiss her ear she reaches up and slings her arms around my neck.

I wet my thumb and trace her hollows, her underarms, her nostrils, her navel, then the birthing scar again. As she sighs I raise her gown. She releases me so I can slip it off. I leave it bunched above her breasts, framing her within her own reflection; and she sees her many colors—her copper hair, her custard skin, the trail of purple bruises on her neck and rippled stomach, between her legs the coils of deepest nigger black.

She turns around and kisses me, tipping up with girlish glee. She hugs me tightly and I watch her in the mirror, her spine drawn tight inside her body, pulling down her shoulder blades. She tongues my nipple through the fabric of my yellow cotton shirt, then drops herself against her heels, thudding on the wooden floor, now rubbing hard against me, her bottom sucking in then flaring out. Something spurts inside me every time I see her underlying fatness pool then drain below her skin.

Naked now, we kiss. Our bodies damp with sweat, we shine each other slowly with our palms. All of this in silence. She turns around and plants her palms against the dresser, reaches down between her legs and finds me.

"We may never fuck like this again," she whispers. "We may never fuck again at all. But this is what it is—a fuck. And this is what I want."

"There is nothing wrong with that."

"Mark me though."

"I marked you yesterday. You have a husband."

"That is my concern. I fucking said to mark me."

She opens up and sucks me down inside her. I am plunging into water. I stroke but there's no bottom. I cannot sense a shore. I am driftwood in the sea until she puts a knee up on the dresser, and I watch with shortened breathing as the bones along her spine begin to twist to find the angle that will lift her cervix.

"Beat me," she whispers. "Beat me, Tuareg. Beat me. Let me feel like I've been kidnapped from my tribe."

The socialist inside me wants to have a conversation. The dramatist inside me wants to play.

I unroll my locks and use them as a cat o' nine. I pull and twist her hair and flog her like a slave . . . on her back and side and down her leg. We grunt. We curse. We call each other dirty names.

Later, as we lay in bed, we kiss again and laugh. She says that I am the man that she would sleep with on her final night on earth. I tell her that I'd choose her as the woman.

It's a lie.

The truth is that she wouldn't choose me either. And she knows this. But she is a woman of experience. And she understands that love affairs are like great dramas. The actors say their lines with all the nuance and conviction that is burdensome in daily life.

A life of full emotion is exhausting.

Affairs, like plays, have running times. In the morning, she will leave for California. I will leave for South Carolina. From there I will return to New York.

The play will continue. Other people will be cast in our roles.

● CHAPTER TWO

The sun is still low when I return to my hotel. Chadwick and the TV crew are staying somewhere else. I lead a lustful life, so I have special needs for privacy.

Poonky Bear is a brilliant idea, a scattering of cottages on terraced land that rises steeply from the sea. Set on stilts and made of wood, with second-floor verandas, the cottages are cooled by brightly colored ceiling fans and rows of louvered doors that open on to ferns and palms and soaring trees festooned with snaking vines and Spanish moss.

As I leave a wooden footbridge and continue in the shade of overhanging trees, I see ahead of me the brick and mortar house of Poonks and Papa Bear. The second floor was damaged in a hurricane no living person recollects. It has never been repaired.

Poonks is white and Papa Bear is black, but they are both Jamaican, thirty-something people on their second marriage—bravely optimistic. Their roofless second floor is now a garden, and as I pass the house wet moans of love come flooding through an open window, mixing with the morning light.

I fall asleep on my veranda, and wake up after nine to call Kwabena, whom I met when I was teaching theater at St.

Regis, an Episcopalian college with a large endowment in rural Minnesota.

Kwabena's voice is lushly southern. He is a tall man, at six-two almost as tall as I am, well defined from years of basketball but thin as a wisp of smoke.

"Is this Mr. Small or Mr. Big?"

"Definitely Mr. Big," he replies. "I called you this morning. Did you get my message?"

"The front desk girls were sleeping when I made it in."

"What time does your flight get in again?"

"It leaves Kingston for Miami at two. From Miami it leaves at three–three-thirty. Gets to you at five."

"I've organized a delegation from the Foolish Virgins of the Confederacy to meet you. It's a southern custom. That is how we welcome our prodigal sons."

As we laugh, I visualize his hazel eyes, his goatee, and his cashew-colored skin.

"Nazia and the kids are dying to see you, man. Don't miss any planes or anything."

"I'll arrange a wake-up call."

"The same wet one you had this morning?"

"I don't even know what you're talking about."

"You are such a classic, man. Don't you ever change."

"I'll tell you when I see you."

Kwabena is a Christian, a Pentecostal who believes in hellfire and the rapture, but he is not a prude. We have an unspoken agreement. He is my conscience and I am his cock. I tease him with a little information.

"Before I left this morning Amaranta anointed me, reached between her legs and passed her sticky hand across my brow and said the benediction."

"You are such a freak," Kwabena whispers. I can tell that Nazia is close. "You shouldn't be allowed near people's children."

"What about their wives?"

"Mine has a razor with your name on it."

"The one she used to cut away your balls?"

"I have four children. How many do you have? And I know you'd have some if you could—just to get the tax relief."

From somewhere in the distance comes the sound of bells.

"Are you going to church today?"

"Not for service. I'm in rehearsal. A one-act thing I wrote about the Ethiopian eunuch who was christened by St. Paul."

"Good. I'll come to see it."

"You haven't been inside a church in ninety-seven years. But I'm also doing a production of *The Tempest* at the county jail in Greelyville. That you need to see. All the members of the cast are prisoners. Talent like you've never seen."

I take my breakfast—orange juice and thick banana porridge—in the little kitchen garden, which is trellised overhead with twigs and hung with mobiles made from copper wire twisted in the shape of fish.

The church bells ring again. The waiter glances at his watch. It is ten o'clock. I motion him to sit with me. He smiles and leans against an iron chair. He's short and slim with beaded braids whose tightness tug his eyes. His tie-dyed shirt is stencilled with his name—Everton Williams.

"Mr. Williams," I ask, "do you know somewhere in Port Antonio that's really good for lunch? Not Bonnie View or Demontevin. I've already been to those."

"In town itself?" He taps his tar-charred lip. "Well, a woman name Rozettewithazed run a little guesthouse and restaurant name Jambalaya right round the corner from Demontevin. From how I see you I think you woulda like it. Is what I woulda call a ole house but what you woulda maybe call quaint. Reasonable, too. I don't exactly know the prices, but I hear is reasonable."

"Her name is Rozettewithazed?"

"No, her name is Rozette, but she always says 'with a zed' when she introduce herself so that people don't spell her name with an *s*. Everybody know her as Rozettewithazed. She is a actress, too. You saw this show *Mighty Quinn* with Denzel Washington? Is down here it flim, y'know. She was in that. And she was in this other flim *Club Paradise* with this guy here, Robin Williams."

I think I know the woman. I ask him to describe her.

"Black, but not quite as black as you."

He covers his mouth. I shrug.

"She tall," he resumes. "Strong back and big-chested."

"Rose Gabidon."

He claps his forehead.

"So she use to name so before *Cocktail*. She was in that, too, with Tom Cruise. She even talk in that one."

Everton is off until the afternoon, so I invite him to come with me. When I pick him up in Drapers he is standing with a knot of men beneath a guava tree, their bodies as strong and dark as coffee—but valued less per pound. There is little work for them outside a hotel or a canefield. They are boys who know the grief of men. Men frozen in the glee of youth.

As we pass a billboard advertising river rafting, I present the situation that I gave to Chadwick yesterday.

Everton would read the bible—Genesis, so he could see how much he'd strayed from God's ideal. Last meal would be okra and snapper with yellow yam and a bottle of Irish moss. Last song would be "Renking Meat" by Ninjaman. He'd have dinner with Iceberg Slim and sleep with porn star Janet Jacme.

With a nervous laugh he turns the question back on me. Which woman would I choose? The truth is that I do not know.

We come around a bend to find a herd of cattle in the road. And as we stop to give them time to cross, the lowing of a choir and the murmur of a Hammond organ bleed between the thorny spaces of a hedge of clotted roses that surround a little concrete church. And I find myself enmired in the mystery and the magic of the blues. And as I sit here waiting, an image starts to form . . . a face . . . a woman's face . . . a face without a face . . . a guitar . . . the blues. A woman . . . a guitar . . . the blues. A woman, a guitar, the blues. Awomanaguitartheblues.

Then, as the ruined Folly Great House comes into view, the memory of the woman comes to me.

Seven years ago I became infatuated with a woman, a woman I have never met. I saw her on a videotape, this woman in a low-cut sequined dress playing some acoustic blues . . . a woman with short hair . . . and there was something peculiar about her face . . . I can't remember what right now—I guess there is something peculiar about everyone's face—but I can see her, her eyes closed, her lower lip tucked in, embroidering an epic of yearning and seduction from the strings of her guitar. I don't know anything about her except that she had short hair and played an Ovation . . . like the one that Marley stroked in "Redemption Song." I don't know which concert this was or where it took place. I haven't thought about her in a very long time.

But she would be the one.

CHAPTER THREE

Port Antonio slides toward the ocean in a corrugated stream of wood-and-concrete houses. Quaint, sleepy, and drained of brightness by the sun, it is every clichéd painting of a Caribbean town: the brick courthouse, the narrow streets, the bungalows with shingled roofs, the porches with contrasting trim.

On The Hill, the bluff that cuts the harbor into east and west, old houses call to mind the Garden District of New Orleans. Exclusive till the sixties, The Hill is slightly mangy now, the kind of place that would attract a tribe of artists in the States.

Jambalaya is a triple-decker, pumpkin-colored clapboard house with lattice-trimmed verandas and a peeling roof.

As we pull up in the bushy yard the woman with the bangles parks her truck beside us. A spliff is clamped between her lips. She is wearing a construction hat, the brim of which is low against her brow. The back is high up on her head, above her braided ponytail.

The ravaged truck, the helmet, the spliff as macho as a thick cigar, they soften me then harden me, weaken then inspire me, electrocute me with desire like the village girl who wishes to be kidnapped by the young guerrilla. *I have to go and brutalize these lazy men that work for me.* What kind of woman says a thing like that?

She is listening to Peter Tosh, the spliff between thumb and forefinger, softly punching through the smoke, lips pursed, lids drawn low, sinking then rising in her seat.

"Were those your men at Rafter's Rest?" I interrupt.

She looks but does not answer.

Everton and I begin to walk toward the restaurant, listening for her footsteps.

"Those were my men," she offers as she passes us. "The lazy lot of them."

"You need a worker man? Then talk to me."

She stops and turns around.

"But can you handle the work?" she challenges. She is smiling with her eyes, appraising me: my orange shirt with cuffs undone, my faded jeans, my sandals.

I am appraising her as well: her double-stranded necklace made of trade beads, her simple yellow cotton dress with fringes just below the knees.

Decisions are being made without discussion. If I say the right thing she will choose me. For what, I am not sure.

She reaches back and languidly unbraids her hair. Her underarms are stubbled. Her skin is what I call foundation brown, the brown of earth after a rainfall, of tamarind seeds, of Guinness stout with milk.

"Can I have a bit of that?"

She hands the spliff to me.

"You want just a piece?" she answers. "Why not take the whole thing?"

I kiss the spliff and give it back. She laughs and walks away, knock-kneed and flat-footed.

"Hey."

She stops and turns around.

"Are you here to eat?"

"To do some business," she replies.

"A business lunch?"

"Just business. And what are you about?"

"Business . . . definitely business."

"I thought you were looking for work. You are not a worker man. You're just another businessman. Businessmen come easy."

"What's your name, boss lady?"

"Frances," she replies. "Frances Carey. And you?"

"Carey. Carey Francis."

"Really?" She cocks her head and laughs with both her mouth and eyes. "Your name is really Carey Francis?"

"I am kidding," I reply. "My name is Carey McCullough."

She shakes my hand. I've worn her down. We walk toward the restaurant. Everton gives us room. He lags behind.

As I reach the porch I hear the sound of thunder: "Carey McCullough! Carey McCullough! What the rass you doing here?"

I glance inside the crowded room.

"Up here, man. Up here!"

Rozette is on the balcony.

Doof, doof, doof. She bounces down the outer stairs, her bulk concealed beneath a gold kimono, her hair cut close to the scalp.

All around us, wait staff in floral shirts are bearing bamboo trays of curried goat and fish filets to tables draped in lace, trailing scents of cumin, thyme, and garlic.

"So where you know him from?" Rozette says to Frances.

"I met him in the parking lot."

"And, Carey, who is this? Your friend?"

"Williams is the name," Everton says. "Everton Williams."

"Rozette," she replies. "Rozettewithazed. So what brings you here, Carey? Lunch?"

I glance at Frances.

"Business . . . work . . . work . . . business."

"You are just as mad as ever."

It is always fascinating when you hear your history being told by someone else. It is very much like watching a production of your play in a foreign country, the way the actors stress the lines in what you thought were unimportant places. Memory is a dialect.

Over lunch on the back veranda of Rozette's living quarters, a converted carriage house behind the restaurant, Frances listens to Rozette's interpretation of my life and gathers that although I speak and understand Jamaican patois fluently, I am American. That I arrived here in 1972 from Cuba, where my family had gone to live when I was five years old. That my father, the Muslim, was an ordained Episcopalian priest. That my mother, the doctor, was a communist and a writer, the daughter of Jamaican Jews. That on Saturdays and Fridays Carey went to synagogue. That on Sundays Carey went to church. That during the week he went to school. That after school he went around the island to the canefields with his mother, teaching workers first aid and how to read and write in Spanish—ratooning revolution. That Carey was an awkward boy.

Frances, I discover, runs a small construction firm from an office in a hamlet in the hills surrounding Kingston. She's a vegetarian, apolitical, and prefers poetry to fiction. Familiar with the properties of herbs and plants, she doesn't wash her face with soap. Instead she uses aloe, cerasse bush, and vinegar. She reads her horoscope religiously and believes in quackish practices like tarot cards and palmistry. She has a mannish side. She repairs her truck herself and often works beside her crew, mixing mortar, breaking stones and cutting reinforcing steel. From her accent she is upper middle class, but her speech is flecked with patois. She doesn't shave or trim her body hair but pays attention to her nails.

Her contradictions, her assurance, her laughter, her voice, they draw me in. She is a character I wish that I had written.

. . .

After lunch we gather in the living room: two love seats across a coffee table centered with a vase of ferns and orange bougain-villea. Frances sits with me. Everton joins Rozette.

"So what brings you to Jamaica, Carey?" Rozette wants to know. We're drinking some Australian wine—shiraz. I summarize the show as a "little TV thing." She presses and I tell her.

"Oh, I know that show," she says. "I didn't know my friend was large like that."

I laugh and shrug it off.

"You're a writer?" Frances asks. She nods. Have I fit a preconception?

Rozette declares: "He's a big important playwright. Just the other day he won a what-you-call-it, Drama Desk award for *Prophet Without Honor*, this play about Garvey and repatriation. And the only reason that he didn't get the Tony was because he didn't choose me for the costar. Me! The one who taught him to project his voice in drama club. Frances, you never hear about it?" Frances says no. "It soon turn into a movie, rumor has it. This time he'll use his head and cast me in the part of Amy Jacques."

"To really show the world how great you are, Rozette, I'll change the part of Amy Jacques to Jacques Cousteau and have you play a man."

This seems to settle her. She begins to pay attention to her wine, but like a geyser she erupts again.

"So like how you are a top celebrity man, you're dating anybody big and famous?"

I glance at Frances.

"No."

Frances takes a sip of wine and folds her arms. Is this what she wants to hear?

"Carey, I am like your sister," Rozette urges. "You mean, a

superstar like you with a national endowment for the punny arts can't find a famous actress or a model to flex with?"

Frances taps my feet. I feel a rush. We are colluding.

"I am actually quite small, Rozette. My publicist creates the hype."

Frances leans away and quips, "You wear a size thirteen."

"That doesn't mean a thing," Rozette replies, dragging deeply on her Dunhill. "I've met some men with some big-big feet and some beenie-beenie buddy. Carey has a big dick, though. A friend told me this one time. Says he can really work it, too."

I laugh and suck my teeth. Inside I am embarrassed.

"So you are bad in bed is what you're saying?" Frances prods. Her gaze is flitting from my face across the flowers to Rozette.

I rest my foot against her instep. She begins to speak. I press it harder. She obeys. I am aroused by this discovery, that she is weak to bold displays of strength and power.

"Okay, Frances and Rozette, it is time to tell the truth. Everton and I are a team. He is big and I am small. I am for before, he is for during, and I am for after. So this is how it works, Rozette. I'll take you for the picnic by the river and stash the wine beneath the stones and sit with you and talk with you and weave you garlands from wild flowers. When evening comes I'll take you home and make your bath and scrub your back and dry you off and oil your skin. And when I'm done I'll test you with my finger. If you're wet and showing other signs of estrus then I'll ring for Everton, who will arrive in due course to hammer and dent your diaphragm. When the bedroom bully leaves, I'll bring you something cool to drink and rub your back and stroke your brow and read you poems—some Neruda or Guillén."

Rozette dares me now: "But there is one way to solve this rass here, Carey. Take it out and show me."

Frances laughs. Everton bows and shakes his head.

"There are too many people here," I joke. "One on one it would be different."

"Okay. Just show it to Frances then. I can always call my friend and she'll remind me. And why Everton is feeling me up as if I have no feelings, I will never understand."

Everton has reached behind the seat and now his hand is on her breast. She turns to look at him. He does not move. Drunk, she takes the dare and kisses him.

I turn to look at Frances, who is smiling with her eyes. I jostle with my zipper. She winks and tilts her head toward Rozette and shrieks.

Rozette turns without releasing Everton's lip. She pats him as he grunts and holds his face and points to Frances then to me.

"Did you see it? Did you see it?"

"No, I missed it," Frances says. "He caught me off my guard."

"Isn't he just a crazy boy?" Rozette replies.

"Insanely mad," says Frances.

"If you still had your band you could write a song about him. 'The Crazy Carey Blues.'"

And as I look at Frances now, a hazy image starts to form . . . the blues . . . a face . . . a woman's face . . . a face without a face . . . a guitar . . . the blues. A woman . . . a guitar . . . the blues. A woman, a guitar, the blues. Awomanaguitartheblues. Her nose doesn't fit her face. It's almost Arabic.

"How long have you had your locks now, Frances?"

"Four years, maybe. Could be five."

"I need to speak to you."

Outside, beneath a mango tree, I stand and face the woman I would sleep with on my final night on earth. The wind is still but there is a natural mystic blowing through the air.

"I have seen you before."

She raises her brows.

"Oh, really? Tell me more."

Her arms are crossed. One foot is cotched up on a white-washed stone.

"I glimpsed you yesterday at Rafter's Rest. But that is not what I am talking about. I saw you on a videotape, like seven years ago. You were playing in a band."

I describe the setting. She tells me it might have been a festival in Negril. Perhaps a simple gig in a hotel. That whole life of music is behind her. She does not remember it or talk about it anymore.

"I hadn't thought about it for a while, myself," I tell her.

"I've learned a couple of things in life," she says. "And one of them is this: We remember the important things in life when we need them."

She looks away. I hold my gaze. I wait until she looks again. She shrugs. We are both aware that the mood has changed, that we have arrived at a point beyond which we know it isn't safe to go. Our voices grow soft until there is nothing left but silence.

"I have also learned some things in life," I tell her as she walks away. "A wise man accepts defeat with grace."

But twenty minutes later, as she walks toward her truck, Frances finds me waiting.

Smiling as she shakes her head, she pauses at her door, inviting me to speak. There are two vehicles between us—her old gray truck and my yellow rented jeep.

When a woman wants you she will let you know. When her feelings ripen she will fall. But I have no time to water Frances Carey. I am leaving here tomorrow on a very crucial mission, to interview Kwabena for the *Sunday Times*.

"Everton," I whisper at a volume she can hear, "ask the lovely and charming Frances Carey if she has a sister that is just as nice as she."

She makes a play of being surprised when Everton lifts a hand to cup his mouth.

●

"Hello please," he improvises, "this is a message for the lovely and charming Frances Carey. My eminent boss, Mr. McCullough, would like to know if perchance you might possibly have in your estimated family a sister sibling who might probably be quarter as nice as you ... y'know ... cyaah ketch Quaashie yuh ketch im shut."

She answers him. He turns to me. Pretends to whisper: "No. She don't."

I give him a message.

He turns to her: "Do you think that in the present or near future that the lovely and charming Frances Carey might possibly, under the right circumstances, like a dreadlocks with the surname McCullough a little bit more than a friend?"

She answers him. He turns to me: "Might be possible ... maybe ... depends."

He turns to her: "Is okay that the lovely and charming Frances Carey isn't sure if she like Mr. McCullough; because Mr. McCullough like the lovely and charming Frances Carey enough for the two of oonoo."

She answers him. He turns to me: "Ha-ha. Big sexy laugh. Thank you very much."

He turns to her: "Is the lovely and charming Frances Carey reachable by phone?"

She answers him. He turns to me: "Yes."

He turns to her: "Can a Rastafarian leftist with a small penis who really likes the lovely and charming Frances Carey call the lovely and charming Frances Carey to tell the lovely and charming Frances Carey that that same, said dread really like her?"

She answers him. He turns to me: "It's up to the particular dread."

He turns to her: "Come wid de digits."

She answers him. He turns to me: "The lovely and charming Frances Carey is listed in the book."

CHAPTER FOUR

She leaves us in the parking lot. I linger for a while, think of her, inhale her fumes, then do what I have done with her for seven years—endeavor to forget.

As we leave the slope that leads us back to town, Everton interrupts my thoughts. We have passed behind the courthouse. Ahead of us, above the trees, the spire of the parish church is rushing sunward like a marlin.

"So you used to live in Cuba," Everton begins. From his tone he is equally intrigued and suspicious.

On our left the harbor stretches in a languid curve. On our right are houses caught in waves of land that rise up into mountains.

"Uh-huh."

"They used to have a party cruise that go from here to Santiago. One time I had a chance to get a job on it. But I didn't have the heart."

He giggles, a bit embarrassed.

"I just got a feeling," he hedges, "like if Castro seize the ship, what I would do."

"He has better things to occupy his time."

He absorbs my answer then replies: "So is escape you escape?"

"No."

"But how you feel about the communist thing?" he challenges. "Personally?"

"A more important thing is how do you feel about the capitalist thing? I no longer live in a communist country. What has capitalism done for you? Personally?"

He rubs his chin.

As he pools his thoughts he asks another question: "So you still can talk the lingua?"

"Speak Spanish? Of course."

"What day I heard you talking it. One night I came to take the dishes from outside and I heard you like you was bussing a lingua."

I am not sure what he means. Amaranta is Brazilian. Perhaps he heard some Portuguese.

"But back to my question," I resume. "What has capitalism done for you? In Cuba, blood, a man like you, an ordinary man, can be the captain of a ship. Here in Jamaica an ordinary man like you will go on that ship as a waiter and leave that ship as a waiter. That is the truth. And the thing is that you have a greater ambition. But a system is keeping you down. That system has a name. Capitalism. That system has a name. Colonialism. That system has a name. The church."

He chuckles.

"Careful how you mention church on Sunday, rasta. God don't take day off."

As we laugh, his suspicion gives way to something more engaging, and he shows himself to be a seeker.

He is curious about the nature of God . . . curious and confused. He has been reading, but reading badly. Sometimes I wonder if it would be better if he had not read at all. His brain is filled with reference books—from the self-important titles, I suspect they are self-published—*The True Nature of the Higher Nubian God Self* by Dr. The Honorable Prophet Methuselah

Jabar ... *From Venus to Cairo to Atlantis: How the Black Race Inscribed the Universe* by Minister Phoenicius Herod Jones.

Someone has poured oil in Everton's gas tank. Before he can move forward he must be drained.

"So what about you?" he asks eventually. "Are you a true rastaman or what?"

"It depends on what you mean by 'or what?' "

Up ahead a woman selling knickknacks from a wood-and-bamboo stall begins to edge out in the road, a lacquered starfish in her hand. When she skips away I realize that the question has provoked me into speeding.

"Okay," says Everton. He swivels toward me, puts his back against the door. "You have the locks and everything ... but ... let's put it this way. You believe that Haile Selassie was God?"

Should I say yes or no? If I say yes and he assumes that I believe in God in a literal way then he will misunderstand me.

I believe that gods are symbols, dreams of perfection that inspire us to reach toward our highest selves.

"So he was God, you think?" he asks again.

"No, I don't believe that."

He begins to nod self-righteously.

"Oh, for you is like a style."

I become a bit defensive now.

"Oh, it's much, much more than that."

"Oh, you do it for the girls."

He flips his hand. I give him five and laugh him off. He would not understand.

As we leave the town behind and forest crowds the road on either side, he tells me: "Turn, please, when I tell you. I want to go by my grandmother."

. . .

The horn disturbs a flock of hens that scatters in a cotton tree to roost. The yard is clumped with razor grass. The fence has missing posts.

A thin old lady, tall with gray plaits hanging past her bosom, pulls herself to the door. Her knees are knots. Her thighs are lengths of rope. She is suffering from arthritis. She seems older than the wooden house, which is blue and white with broken trim and cotched up on white stones.

"Bwai mek yuh nein kum back yah weh day?" she asks in patois. "Me nebba see pickney tan bad lakka yuh."

"Easy, Granny," Everton says. "Is a whole heapa work down at the hotel. Today is the first day off I get in a long time, and see it deh, me come look fe you."

Inside, the house is filled with colored candles. A hundred, two hundred perhaps. All of them are lit and yet the single room is dark. The furniture is sheathed in plastic.

This kind of negro poverty disturbs me. I wait outside. What happened to the revolution?

Everton returns in minutes with the reason for the stop, a portrait of Haile Selassie.

The painting is small. The canvas is caked with dirt and grime. His Majesty is sitting on his throne of gold, his lions at his feet, the King of Kings, the Lord of Lords, the Conquering Lion of the tribe of Judah, a direct descendant of King David through the line of King Solomon and the Queen of Sheba, the head of the Ethiopian Orthodox Church, the oldest Christian Church in the world.

His eyes are meditative. His mouth is serene. The curve of his nose, edged with silver, is glinting like a sword.

In his presence I feel a fullness of joy. If a black man can be anything, including a symbol of the Divine, then why, dear Jesus, not him?

"You're selling it?"

I cannot read the artist's name.

"Three thousand," he replies.

"U.S. or Jamaican?"

"Uncle Sam."

"I have to think about that."

"If you don't want it for yourself, get it for your new girl, Frances. She is a dreadlocks, too."

A vein begins to worm along my temple. Frances Carey. What is she doing now? And what does she believe beyond the tarot cards and palmistry? What sustains her in her time of need?

Back at Poonky Bear, I change into my trunks and go down to the little beach and lie down on the sand, which is powdery and hot. The beach is framed by rocky headlands. The wind comes whistling through.

There is no one here except the lifeguard. The red lounge chairs are empty. In the eastern sky gray clouds advance in convoys like fat galleons.

I unwind my hair and dive into the water, pull and kick against the current, warming my blood against the cold. Beyond the headlands now, in open water, I flip and kick toward the bottom, touch the ridges in the sand and dolphin kick toward the light.

To the west, along the coastline, is a rock, perhaps two miles away. I roll onto my back, pull toward it, the sun pressing on my forehead like a copper penny.

Back inside my room, I change into pajamas, close the doors and try to meditate. The swim has opened me . . . my pores . . . my lungs . . . my mind. Still I cannot find a place of peace. She haunts me.

As I lie in bed, trying to distract myself by following the patterns on the slowly spinning ceiling fan, the telephone rings.

"My grandmother want to see you," Everton says after the courtesies. "She say she was deep in her meditation and she get a message for you."

"So she's working at the front desk now."

"You know old people and they science," he says through a laugh.

"So what does she have to tell me?"

"She didn't say. She just say for you to come."

"Why not? I need a good distraction."

When I arrive she motions me with wrinkled hands.

"Sit down," she says in a quiet voice. She is facing me across a small Formica table, squatting on a stool. The candles in the room are pulsing. Still the room is dark. The air is thick as if I'm sitting in a cloud of carbon dust. It is hard for me to breathe.

"I am glad you came," she says, tracing circles on her red-and-purple tunic. With her thumb she dots her forehead, chest, and shoulders. The pulsing flames create an optical illusion. I think I see the contours of a shimmering cross. "You should always come when the spirit calls you."

This is not the voice I heard this afternoon. She's speaking English, not patois. Her pronunciation is nonstandard but unplaceable, like a person raised outside her place of birth.

I listen to her politely. When she is done I lay some bills out on the table. She waves her hand. I shake my head. We do this back and forth until she counts them.

Returning from her house I come around a bend to find a man directing traffic wearing water boots and dungarees, flagging with a crimson panty tied up on a bamboo pole, laughing at the joke. A flatbed truck is trying to turn around. I will have to wait. His attitude reminds me of the men at Rafter's Rest, which makes me think of Frances once again. No. This is not true. The memory does not make me think of Frances. It is coincidental— like a leaky faucet synchronizing with the rhythm of a song.

"Hello, may I speak to the lovely and charming Frances Carey, please?"

I have called her.

"Who the person?"

"Tell her Carey McCullough."

"Miss Frances on the road, sir. You are the man from the block factory?"

Should I lie or tell the truth? I bluff and tell her yes.

"She cannot come today again. She broke her axle in Port Antonio. She not coming in tonight."

"Well, I have some business to discuss with her."

A bead of sweat rolls down my chest. I slide down in the seat to catch it as I feel it pooling in my navel. "Does she have a cell?"

"Yes, sir. But I can't give it out. Maybe she could call you back."

As I speed along the coastal road I get a call. It isn't Frances. It is Zadie, my assistant. The *Sunday Times* has called again. The profile on Kwabena is severely overdue.

"Carey, the deadline was three months ago."

"I know. I know. I know."

"Then how come it isn't done?"

Because, I want to say, Kwabena's genius frightens me. Because I feel quite small around him. If this world were fair or if Kwabena were ambitious he would be the one on *Trapped in Transit*.

When I return to Poonky Bear there is a note beneath the door that opens to the kitchen garden:

You might not come back from granny yet. She take long sometimes, depending on the spirit. If is rum she go fast. If is gin she take her time. Your girl Frances just check in by the way. Think you might want to know. A saw the taxi bringing her. The front desk girl said her van break down. Maybe Selassie really have the power. I make the front desk put her in the cottage right over you. Look up and you will see it.

Through the twigs that form the trellis I observe her. She is sitting in a window, looking out to sea, cutting and shuffling a deck of cards.

There is so much that she does not know.

When I saw her for the first time, seven years ago, I was trying to kill myself.

I had driven nonstop from New York to Columbia, trying to reach Kwabena, trying to get to him before the metastatic guilt inside me crushed my will completely, pushing me to plunge into the belly of a truck.

But half a mile away, as the front wheels took the grade that led onto the final exit ramp, I surrendered to the sadness and I stopped the car and walked across the interstate, head thrown back, arms outstretched, begging for release.

I don't remember how I reached Kwabena's house. I must have walked. I had received a glancing blow. The driver did not stop. My skull was cracked. Two ribs had snapped. I dragged a leg behind me like a broom.

In my confusion I believed that I had died.

According to the stories that were told to me, Kwabena was the first to reach the door. But when he saw me he was stunned.

He could not move. I could not think. I stumbled through the alcove to the living room, where all was quiet. Nazia later told me she was screaming. All was quiet then I heard a ringing noise and saw a flash and then the ceiling framed by jagged glass. I had collapsed against the coffee table, and in trying to orient myself had rolled beneath it.

Then as I tried to raise myself I saw her, Frances Carey, singing on TV. And something in that moment made me want to live.

All that I am I owe to her. Frances saved my life.

CHAPTER FIVE

Upstairs in my room now, flung across the bed, I gaze out through a window at the sky. The darkened clouds are purple-gray like bruises. A peaty smell begins to rise up from the earth. Perhaps the worms are turning.

I feel as if a tongue of iron is suspended from my throat. There is a pain against my side as if my heart is pealing on my bones.

I close my eyes. I call Rozette. From behind my lids I sense a flash and hear a crack of light igniting thunder. My world is at war.

"So tell me," I begin when Rozette answers. "Who's this Frances Carey?"

The rain begins to crackle the connection. I lean my head from side to side, roll across the spread, trying to catch and hold it. Every time I pick it up it slips me like a dish retrieved from soapy water. Every time it falls it shocks me like the crashing of an heirloom.

I move to the veranda, lips and nipples puckered, watching great trees rocking like a Pentecostal choir, thrashing in a wind invisible but moving like the Holy Ghost.

Who is this Frances Carey?

This is what I think I know . . . this is what I've put together from a conversation broken into shards.

The lovely and charming Frances Olivia St. Margaret Carey is not Jamaican.

She was born in Guyana on February 11, 1963, and came to live in Jamaica with her father in 1981, at the age of seventeen, after a cataclysmic argument with her mother.

Her mother is an import-export trader. Her father teaches law. Frances speaks to neither.

Headstrong. Loyal. Clever. Shrewd. This is how she was when Rozette met her.

Open. Helpful. Happy. Cool. This is how she is today.

We would get along, Rozette believes. I ask her why. Her answer piques my interest even though it angers and embarrasses: "She fucks without good sense or reason."

Like the man who makes a show of breathing deeply to deny the odor of his body gases, I indulge Rozette, wincing as I fight the burning in my lungs.

"She is really funny," says Rozette. "She'll go a long time without any man at all, and then is just man-man-man-man-man-man-man like man going outta style. Two, three, four, five, six man in her life one time . . . especially when she was in music. . . . She would have a man with every meal. . . . She would take their balls for multivitamins. But she not so hot today. She says she getting in tune with her soul nowadays. But that won't last for long. No . . . I shouldn't say that. She's my friend."

"What should you say?"

"That she is learning to settle down. She used to be wild nuh rass, y'know. Let's put it this way. One time she used to have to have three, four, five, six, seven things going one time—used cars, graphic design, catering, import-export, landscaping. But just like with men, she settle down. This construction thing now is like three years old and she doing really well with it. Keeping her busy though. You don't see her on the road again."

I close my eyes . . . observe myself . . . see my face defined by muscles tightened up in lines of anger . . . lines of anger complicated by the web of veins that drain the steaming blood from my erection.

Why so many lovers? What were they like? What did they give her? Were these affairs between equals? Or was she considered a whore?

Whore. The roundness of the word creates the image of a droplet. In my head I see a photograph of Frances. The droplet seeps behind the glass, stains the paper, turns it brown, despoils it.

I put my feet up on the banister, ease back on the chair, admitting a truth to myself.

There is something that excites me in the dirty girl, in the woman who's been trampled through and used . . . a softness in the will . . . a slackness in the hip . . . a willingness to please in bed that rises up to meet my need to hose away the odor of the hordes of men who've sweated in her folds. Call it my perversion. But I like to feel within myself the power to redeem. Ironically, I've yet to find my own redemption.

Whore. In my mind I see the photograph again. Now the brown has been romanticized to sepia. And Frances is reclining in a tub of soapy water.

Making love to her must be a sweet indulgence . . . an affair with her a thing of simple beauty. No problems. She understands that sex is not a bond but a release.

CHAPTER SIX

The rain subsides. Jets of sunlight spray the clouds, dispersing them like suds, revealing a ceramic sheen, a bright Islamic blue.

Now I feel my thoughts being drawn beyond the banister, across the trees, beyond the shore and the horizon, to the edge of memory ... to a house, a concrete house with Moorish arches, a fountain and a Spanish roof, a house on a hill, a house inspired by the mansions of Havana, the house my mother owned in Kingston.

Below the house, on what was once my mother's great-grandfather's orange farm, are the houses of the newly rich: red-wood louvers, flat slab roofs, windows with fringed awnings.

In our house, on our side-faced veranda, behind a wooden lattice screen, my brother holds a test tube to the light. There are flasks and beakers spread out on the floor—blue tiles inlaid with hexagons in white and tangerine.

My sisters are upstairs in the parlor that divides their rooms, watching the helper braid her daughter's hair with hands that stuffed a hen and rubbed black pepper and kosher salt into the gills of fat fish that were delivered still damp with sea water.

Next door, my enemies the Chin Loy brothers plunge into

their pool, their father's whistle pacing them toward another suite of medals at Miami Springs.

On the other side the Dutch ambassador is practicing his serve.

Off the back veranda, in the courtyard, which opens to the garden by an eight-foot wooden gate, I am wearing Puma sweats and Pro-Keds, juggling a tennis ball from knee to knee, a soccer prodigy developing finesse.

I am twelve years old. My brother is sixteen and studious. My sisters are eight and cute. They are all that I'm not.

Their hair is soft like frosting. Their skin is golden brown like flan. They are my father's rich desserts.

There are times when I am patient with my father's complications. This isn't one of them.

My father's father, Pa McCullough, was a doctor, an orphan who was raised in a Christian mission in Accra. Pa McCullough did not know his tribe. English was his only language. Formal in bearing and strict, with a barrel chest and center-parted hair, he studied medicine at Cambridge on a scholarship and, perhaps to escape his past, did not return to Ghana. He was twice married. His first wife was white, and the reason, I believe, that he abruptly caught a steamer from Bristol to New York.

He met his second wife, Ma McCullough, in 1922, when she answered an ad for a domestic. She had recently arrived from Nashville and was a seamstress, a maple-colored woman who insisted that her mother was a Cherokee. She was nineteen when they met and he was forty. When they married he was forty-five.

Their five children were born in Harlem, in a house on Riverside Drive. It was a masonry house with wide arches on squat columns, and windows deeply set into the walls. On one side there was a turret. On the top floor of the turret was the study; there Pa McCullough gave his children extra lessons every day.

For Pa McCullough education had a single purpose—dignity. As an orphan, as a negro, as an African, this vital thing had at one time been withheld from him and he had felt deficient.

SATISFY MY SOUL ● 35

Do you know what you are to the white man? he would ask his children. You are mules. Beasts of burden. How can you be so happy when you are ignorant. Come here, beast children, let me burden you with books.

For his daughters he selected husbands crafted in his image—African doctors schooled in Europe. Thus a standard was created for my father, a future was mapped out.

My father did not make the grade. He applied to Cambridge but he was rejected. Like me, he was weak in mathematics.

However, he was accepted by Columbia. And although Pa McCullough was disappointed, he contributed his blessing. There are times when I believe that my life would have been different if Ma McCullough did not intervene.

Growing up in segregated Tennessee, Fisk had been her dream. It was perhaps America's most prestigious negro school, its negro Yale or Harvard.

Ma McCullough had relatives in Nashville who had expected her to come to nothing in New York. In her mind her son would be the living proof of her success. So she urged him to lie, to tell Pa McCullough that he wanted to leave, that he wanted to build his mind through travel.

Fisk, Pa McCullough told my father, was placed within a negro's reach. Negroes had to learn to stretch beyond. If these negro schools were great, he asked him, why didn't white people send their children there?

Pa McCullough did not attend my father's graduation. Instead he sent a note:

Congratulations. You have shown that you can think. Four years have passed. What are you going to do with your life?

My father became an Episcopalian priest—to his mother's disappointment. She was Pentecostal and had raised her children in the Pentecostal church—although they had been christened

Episcopalian. Pa McCullough was Episcopalian. He had attended an Episcopalian mission school in Ghana, and although he rarely went to church and didn't care about the details of religious practice, he did not trust the vision of the Pentecostal church. In his mind it was a church without real ambition. With so many illiterate people in its congregation, where were its schools?

My father joined the priesthood, I believe, because he thought that it would bring him closer to his father, the man he most admired in the world.

Perhaps to seem more worldly, I believe, he attended seminary overseas, in Canada, a former British colony.

But by the time my mother met my father in the spring of 1958 he was no longer Episcopalian. He was a Muslim, a member of the Nation of Islam.

After seminary school he took a commission in the army and served five years as a chaplain.

He left the army as a lieutenant and moved to Chicago for reasons that I do not know. Perhaps he'd grown tired of trying to please his father. Perhaps he'd heard his father's wisdom in the Nation's call to dignity and self-reliance, had seen his father's wardrobe in the Nation's formal dress.

My mother was a first-year intern at Northwestern when she met him. She was a freethinker and a communist, a rich girl sent abroad to study.

In my father's head my mother was a lush exotic. Her last name was García, and her hair was long and curly, which led him to assume that she was Cuban.

My mother was in fact a Spanish Jew, the daughter of a merchant family that had arrived in Kingston in the mid-1800's after settling first in Cuba.

In her memoir, which was published in the early 1980's, she explained her attraction to my father:

It began as an adventure. I seduced him for no other reason than that he was the most exquisite man I had ever seen. I was fascinated with the Nation of Islam. Not their politics, which was a little, how shall we say, "unique." I was fascinated by the fact that all these handsome men were celibate. Celibacy has always puzzled me. I saw him for the first time at a rally. I saw in his eyes that his will was weak. I paid a little boy to slip him my address. He came to me that night. I let him in. There was an instant understanding that we had no future. No high ideals. No deep affection. He would visit me at night. I would meet him naked at the door. He would reach for me. There would be music. He would dance me to the bed. A drink would be waiting. We would have it. We would screw. There was something in the way he did not fully share himself with me that made me feel dirty, like a whore. And I must admit that I liked that. I had convinced myself of the dignity of prostitutes. I was a feminist. No, I was a fool.

They were together for a year, until a month before her graduation—when she missed her period.

She did not discuss the conversation in her memoir, but this is how I have always imagined it. The setting is a pretty but shambolic studio in Highland Park.

It would have been after midnight. He would have been wearing a fedora and a double-breasted suit. She would have been wearing a dress with short sleeves. Her hair would have been down, to show him, perhaps, that all the news was not gloomy, that, if he wanted her to, she'd have his child.

She would have sat on the bed, arms folded. She would have pointed to a chair and asked him to sit. He would have stood with his feet apart, his hands behind his back, tense and waiting, wondering why she hadn't met him naked at the door.

She would have whispered, biting her lip and nodding her head but smiling always with her eyes. He would have listened absently.

She would have made it clear that if he wanted she would have had the baby. She would have told him that she knew that this would change their lives. She would have told him that she'd be the one to bear the shame, that he didn't have to take the risk— unless he understood this as his duty.

He would have been embarrassed by her offer, by her assumption that he was too small to bear his portion of the blame. And he would have cried. No. He would have wailed.

Crying would have made him a weakling, and being a weakling would have been *his* burden. But wailing would have made the burden hers, for it would have meant that she had asked too much of him, which would have weighed her down with guilt like someone who had been impatient with a sickly child.

My mother would have lain across the bed. She would have held him, rocked him, holding in her hurt and fears, would have hushed him as he whimpered that he always found a way to fail, to disappoint his father.

And as she lay with him my father would have found a way to take advantage of her feelings.

She would have begun to feel his hand along her side. And she would have sighed from disbelief but would have held him tightly out of habit. And she would have shuddered when his snubness pierced her and stiffened as he emptied his frustrations at the entrance to her womb.

She would have held him, absorbed his weight. She would have held it all until she felt as if she couldn't breathe, then she would have blurted out that she didn't know what she was going to do, exposing all her helplessness, giving him the chance to be heroic.

She would have told him that she would understand it if he could not see his child.

He would have promised her that that would never happen. And she would have answered *yes, yes, yes*. And he would have repeated *no, no, no*—and this is when she would have blurted out that she had to seek the counsel of a rabbi. And this is when he would have rolled away from her, mannish now, and straightened up his clothes and said with practiced, focused meanness that he could never father children with a Jew.

And this is when she would have told him to go fuck himself. And this is when he would have learned that he could beat her.

I don't know if this is how it happened. But I am sure of all that followed.

My father confessed his sin and was punished and forgiven in his mosque. My mother left for London to pursue a fellowship, and there she had my brother on her own.

When Pa McCullough was diagnosed with cancer in 1961, he sent a copy of his will to all his children.

The house in Harlem would belong to his first grandson, but his daughters had produced only girls. So my father traced my mother to a little flat in Camden, apologized, made promises, renounced the Muslim faith and convinced her to return with him and be his wife.

They married quietly in Chicago and moved into the house; there, my sisters and I were born.

Like his sisters, my father had married a foreign doctor.

My mother became a celebrity in New York. Her East Village office was a weekend art gallery and nighttime salon for young poets. She had affairs with famous people, most of whom were men, wrote op-ed pieces, drank too much shiraz, and in quick succession published three novels, none of which were good.

Having neither a profession nor a practical skill, and lacking both pride and ambition, my father chose to make his living off the family trust.

When Pa McCullough died in 1962, my father lost his whole identity. Nonetheless he was a man with many names. The priest who married the atheist. The Muslim weakened by the Jew. The brother with the white girl. The negro with the foreign wife.

Then in 1967 he earned another name: the fugitive.

Two weeks after my mother announced that she would run for mayor—more a protest than a dream—my father was named in a conspiracy to smuggle weapons into Attica.

It was obviously a lie. My father was born incapable of action or heroics. We fled without packing.

We went by train to Montreal, by plane to Veracruz, arriving in Havana on a freighter.

In Havana my father found employment as a public denouncer. In many ways he had also found his talent.

With my mother as interpreter, he would mount the stage at rallies dressed in army greens, tall and black with his father's barrel chest, and denounce America and denounce capitalism and denounce racism and denounce religion and denounce all forms of fascist exploitation.

Then later at night, at home in our assigned apartment in a building slapped together by Romanian soldiers, he would go out on the terrace with a long cigar and a bottle of rum, duck beneath the laundry, lean against the rail and denounce the fucking Jewish whore who'd ruined his life, the white bitch who had trapped him, the atheist, the fucking antichrist who hated God.

And we would watch his shadow through the louver blades, grotesque against the drabness of the paintless wall, turning our heads each time we heard the tinkle of the rum against the powder blue enamel mug, listening as our father pissed away his life.

And later we would listen through the bedroom door and hear our mother singing as she rubbed his head: Things will be all right . . . don't worry. As soon as things were right we would be moving to Jamaica. The PNP are socialist at heart and they will win the next election. They will never give us up. My father died and left a home. We're going to be all right. But now is not the time, my love. Now is not the time. But soon, my darling, soon. Don't cry. Everything's gonna be all right. Don't cry, my love. Don't cry.

. . .

I last saw my father seven years ago, at a premiere at the Public in New York. I was directing Lorca's *Blood Wedding*, which I'd launched at the Seattle Rep the year before.

Still I was unsure of how New York would take it—a play directed by a negro, set in Appalachia, exploring what could only be described as Mediterranean passions.

I had not seen my father in fifteen years. I was standing by a column, drinking apple juice with seltzer, counting off the critics as they came, when I noticed him, an old man pacing the floor, striding out toward me, then stopping, snapping his fingers, then turning around, alarmed and disappointed, as if he'd just lost his wallet.

I looked at him. I tried to smile. He clenched his teeth and slowly made his way across the broad terrazzo tiles, his hair now white and low, his shoulders stooped. Like me he wore a navy suit. His was loose and worn. His voice had thinned. He had no face. Instead there was a raisin.

He had been living in Nashville, he volunteered.

I asked him if he needed tickets.

No, no. He glanced over his shoulder. I followed his eyes.

So who is the lady? I asked.

He looked down at his snow-crusted shoes, looked up again and took an interest in my drink.

He began to whisper solemnly. Was I drinking rum? I told him no. He rubbed my back, then shook his head, then squeezed my shoulder. There was silence as I willed him to remove his hand and slip it in his pocket.

So what else had he been doing?

Traveling with his lady friend. And where had they been? Oh, all over Europe . . . Cambridge . . . he'd seen Cambridge and it was everything Pa McCullough had told him and more. Like what? He seemed to have forgotten that I had studied there. He couldn't explain himself. It was clear that he was lying.

I told him that a man must always speak the truth. His eyes began to glow. He asked if I was living right with God. I raised my brows.

Did I know that He's the only truth? Did I know that my mother had been screwing Mr. Chin Loy all these years? Did I know this? And that was why he didn't like me playing with his sons.

I shrugged and asked him if he had a number. He said something in a mumble. I caught a couple of words.

Angry? Who's angry? Your lady friend is angry?

Yes, angry. She's angry.

About what?

That you're not looking after me.

But does she really understand the kind of man you are?

He straightened up, indignant now, and got to what I believe had always been the point—could I lend him eight hundred dollars? He was three months late with his rent.

I glanced at the woman. She was short and soft-bodied like a spoiling fruit. When she turned away from me I noticed that two inches of her zipper were undone.

I gave my father all I had, ninety-seven dollars. I would have hurried to an ATM and taken out the maximum allowed. But this was opening night. I could not leave the building.

When I slipped the folded bills into his palm he clenched his fists and turned his face toward the ceiling, clamped his eyes and blurted out, Praise God.

And I lost my patience. I lost my patience not to anger but to something else. Call it sympathy. No. Call it disappointment.

In a flash of clarity I had realized that my father, at his core, had always been a Pentecostal, that the Episcopalian Church and Islam had been mock rebellions. And I admitted to myself that there was something fundamental in the Pentecostal Church that I despised—a certain undignified glee.

Pentecostals plead with God as if they don't believe that they're entitled to his grace. Episcopalians ask in quiet voices with assurance—they ask *believing* they'll receive.

And there he was, my father, a man who had been given a decent chance in life, oh-lawding like a slave.

Dignity. Dignity. My father had lost his dignity.

As soon as I declared this to myself I felt a need to hug him, to reassure him that for me to give him all I had was not largesse but a simple act of kindness, an example of the kind of grace to which he was entitled as a human being and that I would give him more after the final curtain.

I hugged him. He inhaled wetly and began to tremble as he held his breath. When he let it out I felt him softening, and I palmed his head and placed it on my shoulder.

My father. Oh, my father. He began to speak. I held him tighter. He tried to speak again. I rocked him. Then he jerked away.

My locks had brushed his face.

I pretended not to notice. His face began to twitch. If I turned away, I knew, he would have wiped it.

I asked about my mother. He had not heard from her since she moved to Israel. Be careful of the Jews, he offered, as he glanced around the lobby. Learn from how your mother took me down.

I shrugged. He reached into his pocket for a bible.

People had begun to watch us now. I turned away. He followed me, extending it. I turned around and asked him once again about my mother. He said she was in hell.

I told him that I had to go . . . and would he please accept a pair of tickets . . . for the first time in his life . . . come see what I can do.

He shook his head and smugly told me that he only went to gospel plays. I told him they were rubbish. He laughed and shook his head again.

I told him they were godless. Then I watched in disappointment as an educated man recited that they couldn't be, that they were executive-produced by God.

A gospel play had brought him back to God, my father testified. I told him that he'd never left.

The sarcastic answer shocked him to intelligence, and as people watched us we began to have a calm debate, quietly, in respectful tones, raising a finger to mark our turn to speak . . . until he asked me if my plays were like the rest . . . irrelevant to the soul.

I asked him if he'd ever seen a play by August Wilson? Ed Bullins? Did he remember seeing *A Raisin in the Sun*?

He leaned his head and placed a thumb beneath his chin.

Shange? I continued. Baraka? Soyinka? Césaire? Derek Walcott?

If you want to learn about forgiveness, I told him, if you want to learn about the essence of the Christian faith, see Baldwin's *Amen Corner*, see Fugard's *Master Harold and the Boys*, see Aimé Césaire's *La Tempête*. Leave these rubbish plays alone!

He shook his head and fixed his chin and crossed his arms and laughed.

And I found myself orating in a voice that I admitted had been pilfered from the great denouncer: If you really want to understand the meaning of redemption, the fundamental meaning of grace—in some of the greatest language ever written—fuck the hacks who profiteer from negro ignorance and reach for William Shakespeare. *Macbeth* explores the world of evil and man's need to be rescued by God's power better than any gospel play or any sermon ever preached in any church in this country!

He began to fidget now. And as he tried to reconvene the plot he told me to be quiet. I shook my head and sucked my teeth. He raised his hand, I thought, to slap me. I grabbed his wrist. The money slipped. I picked it up. He groped for it. I held it out of reach.

He looked at me. I looked away, guilty and ashamed—until he punched me. I did not see it coming. The conversation had come to an end and I was turning to walk away when I felt a thud against my side and whipped around to see my father facing me with doubled fists as I had seen him stand astride my mother—and I lunged.

But something shifted deep inside me and my hands fell on his shoulder in a son's embrace.

And what did he do? The fucking bastard punched again.

As I held him tighter I heard inside my head reverberations of my mother's songs of comfort. And the blows began to feel as if they were a part of me, as if I had a second heart, pumping with ancestral blood.

I think of all these things until the rain subsides. Then I will myself to sleep. When I awake the leaves are almost dry.

The mobile rings. It's Frances Carey.

● CHAPTER SEVEN

Her voice is as casual as sex.

"You called me."

"Yes."

"I'm calling back."

"I see."

"It's Frances."

"Of course."

"So what?"

"So nothing."

"So good-bye."

"No, Frances. Wait."

"For what?"

"Why the rush?"

"Oh, stop it, Carey. Things happen in their time."

"I don't understand."

"Then it means you're not ready."

"For what?"

"Oh, Carey, you're *really* not ready."

"Well . . ."

"Why did you call me?"

"To talk."

"But you're not ready to talk. See. You're not ready."

"I am."

"So talk."

"But not right now."

"You are *so* not ready for this."

"For what?"

"For *this*," she emphasizes.

"This what?"

"This talk you say you want to give me."

"Did I say that?"

"Why did you call me?"

"To talk."

"Well, talk."

"I need a few minutes."

"Take them."

"I was in the middle of something."

"I understand. Rain is always romantic."

"Not *that* kind of thing."

"Not *what* kind of thing?"

"The kind of thing you're talking about."

"You know my mind?"

I am a mouse in the jaws of a playful cat. She means no harm, but she is hurting me.

"You're stressed," she says. "You need release. Come and have a drink with me to celebrate the sun."

"Where are you?"

"You know where I am. You were watching me. Come outside and see me clearly now. Trees will be the only obstacles in your way."

"Yes. I know where you are."

"So why did you ask where I am?"

"You could have moved."

"I could have. But I didn't."

"Should I come or are you coming?"

"We're going to Poonks and Papa Bear's for tea."

I arrived at Poonks and Papa Bear's to discover that I'm not expected.

"I'm supposed to be meeting someone here for tea," I say to Poonky when she gets the door.

Poonky's hair was sandy brown two days ago. It's black today. Her face is square. Her chin is short. Her legs are tight and tanned as if she's had a life of swimming pools and riding. Her arms are slim and freckled.

"Who are you supposed to be meeting?" she asks as she leads me through the entrance hall.

It is a house of dark wood and beige caning, of mirrors in old frames, and potted plants with fringed and fronded leaves.

She is wearing chunky slippers. She walks quickly and pivots slightly with each step as if she's mashing insects. Through her blouse I notice that her bra is half-unhooked. I am an intruder.

Upstairs, on the roof garden, she offers me a seat and says, while drawing away, "Frances is like that, you know. Sometimes her thoughts run ahead of her mind."

I look around. At either end are gabled walls. Where the water-damaged plaster has been soaked away, chipped bricks are showing through. Along the sides are rows of empty windows filled with views of trees and sky. An ant is crawling up the stem of a banana tree. My face is being shaded by a potted palm.

Poonky brings me tea, leans back and stretches her arms along the back of the iron bench, smiling at a private thought. There is concertina pleating at the corners of her eyes.

"She's coming," she says when she looks again. "How is your stay?"

"Perfect. I have no complaints."

I put a spoon of sugar in my tea and stir it.

"Is it okay?" she asks abstractedly. She looks toward the stairwell, smiling.

Papa Bear emerges in a gray T-shirt and boxers. He is tall and flesh-wrapped with a head of boisterous hair. He looks healthy in the way of cattle—big-boned with lots of meat.

He shakes my hand and sits beside his woman, who settles in the space reserved for her beneath his arm.

I raise the pot for Papa Bear. He shakes his head politely. None for him.

"So you're here for tea with Frances," Papa says.

I laugh. He makes a face to humor me.

Poonky up against him is a purring cat. He begins to stroke her arm as if it's covered in a shiny coat. She brings her legs around and balls herself into the comfort of his lap. The shorts ride up. I glimpse a ridge of freckled fatness on her hip. It urges me to fill my mouth with bread, chewing slowly as she reaches up and kisses him, simply at first, then with a languid inevitability, slipping her bottom lip beneath his own to suck it like a segment of a tangerine.

"Maybe I should go."

Without parting lips or turning, Poonks and Papa fan their hands and tell me to remain.

Now Papa's hand is on her thigh, limpid in the peaceful rest of ownership.

"You want a spliff?" he asks.

Poonky shuts her eyes and slips her nose beneath his arms. She fills her lungs, inflates her shoulders, and, as Papa rocks her, slowly lets his scent drain out.

She squirms and brings her knee up to his chest, softly presses it against his nipple, and as I reach toward the Altoid tin and take a pinch of herb my mind begins to see them as they would have been if I were absent.

She looks at me in a way that tells me that she knows what I am thinking, that what I think I am thinking is untrue, that I am not thinking about what would have happened in my absence but rather what I'd do with her if she or Papa should invite me.

Now I am embarrassed.

She reaches with prehensile feet and grips my spliff between her toes. As Papa laughs she moves it in a lazy circle, holds it still, waiting. But I am too self-conscious to begin to understand the moment or the meaning. I cannot move. Her legs begin to tremble. I watch her shimmering flesh. The man who assumed my body when I died from shame begins to lean toward her. She slips the spliff inside his nose then makes a circle with her toe around his mouth, leaves her imprint on his bottom lip, laughing as he slinks away.

CHAPTER EIGHT

"What happened, Frances? Where were you?"

"Oh. I'm sorry. Something happened. Are you there?"

"Am I where? Of course I'm not."

"So you are where?"

"You're sounding so unfazed."

"You are sounding so huffy."

"I don't know what to say to you."

"Yes, you do. You should tell me how you feel."

"Where would I begin?"

"So do you want to talk?"

"You know, you could apologize."

"For what?"

"For having me go someplace where you were not."

"But I was just getting ready to leave."

"Well, I'm not there anymore. I'm in my room so it doesn't matter."

She pauses.

"Carey, this is such a different you."

"How can you say this? You don't know me."

"Women know these things."

"Like what?"

"Like when a man is stressed and needs release."

"You are full of . . . something. Something. I just don't know what it is."

"Ask and I will tell you. I am good like that."

"Like how?"

"People tell me all their problems all the time."

"I don't have any problems."

"You are huffy again."

"Well, you're being really difficult, Frances, and frankly speaking, childish. You make a plan with me to meet somewhere. I go. The people have no idea that I'm coming. They . . . well, she lets me in and I have to watch her and her man."

"Watch them doing what?"

"Look, there is nothing like being where you're not needed. I was not supposed to be there. I was clearly interrupting. I mean, what is the meaning of all this? Why did you tell me to meet you somewhere if you knew you weren't going to be there?"

"It slipped my mind. Being childish, well, I sometimes do infantile things like taking important phone calls from the man who's bringing me another car because my van broke down so I can get my ass to Kingston where I have a meeting in the morning with the Minister of Housing who wants to discuss with me the feasibility of designing in conjunction with the government of Holland interior walls made of sugarcane fiber for some low-income housing in his constituency. Now I can find out if and when and how my car is coming or I can go gallivanting. Forgive me for choosing the former, for taking a minute, which admittedly turned into a half hour, to sort out something as important as that." She pauses. "And yes, I said, 'forgive me,' so you have the apology you said you had to have."

Through the phone I hear a slap and then a grunt of disdain. And I know it's not because she has realized that her rant, despite its passion, has severely missed the point.

But the fact that she has missed the point is not for me the point. The point is that although I know that she has missed the point, she has made a point with me. Frances Carey understands that in the mathematics of emotion logic is as simple as arithmetic, and that passion, with its symbols and its metaphors, is algebraic, a higher, deeper form—and further, that like a charismatic teacher with a laggard, she is positioned to inspire me to logic, to her logic, through the simple equations of faith. For now I am convinced that she is right, although I can't explain the reason. The proof is her approval. She leans into the phone and whispers, "Come and talk to me."

Outside now, as I take a gravel trail up to her villa, we continue our conversation in a different mood. In a steady curve the trail ascends along a gully through a stand of trees with interlocking branches. The brown and silver trunks are clumped with green and white bromeliads. Rooted round the trees are shrubs as dense as pubic hair.

My eyes are open yet they're shut. I am walking blindly into love.

My head is now a kitchen where a feast is being prepared. There, all thoughts and sights and sounds have wet commingling scents. We are speaking as we walk, but I don't know in what order, or who is saying what to whom.

"You should have fucked me when we met."

"My hand is in my underwear."

"You are really fucking difficult."

"I can smell myself."

"I am going to make this easy."

"So what does Rozette really think of you?"

"How do you want me to fuck you?"

"I think you like to be hit."

"I think Poonks is really sexy."

"Does she turn you on?"

"Are you bi?"

"I am thinking of your nipples now, sucking them, feeling them grow in my mouth."

"I want the world to know you fucked me. Can I scream your name when you make me come?"

"You make me think of wicked things."

"You make me want to be a saint."

"If you could cook and eat a part of me, what part would you choose?"

"If you had a choice between me and the last person that you slept with would you choose me?"

"I am not bi but I've considered it."

"My ass is tender."

"Tell me that you'll suck my toes."

"Don't come. Don't come. No. No. No. No. Hold it."

"Do you want children?"

"I would roast your shoulders with a salt-and-pepper rub."

"The last woman I was with was really sweet and caring."

"Are you bi?"

"Did you fuck or simply play around?"

"I would eat your ears. I'd sauté them with chanterelles and ginger."

"What now? What now?"

"Will you tell anyone about this?"

"I haven't made love to anyone in months."

"You should know that I am whorish."

"I would have to have the two of you to really say."

"Are you a liar?"

"I have a nasty side."

"Tell me that you love me when I come, okay. Scream it so I'll hear your voice above my scream."

"I'm masturbating. Shit. There is no privacy. Anyone who comes along will see."

"I want a love like Poonks and Papa Bear. A love that fucks the world and rolls along."

"If your ass is really tender, I will soothe it with my tongue."

"I am glad you told the truth, that just like me you fucked someone last night."

"Will you be easy for others? Will you be easy for only me?"

"When I act that way it means I need some loving. Don't fight me then, just love me. Don't love me freely though. Ration it. Make me work for it. Subdue me. I need discipline."

"I didn't sleep with anyone last night. It was a lie. Now tell the truth. Did you?"

"I love you."

"I love you."

"What do you really mean?"

"Love has no meaning."

"Love is like a fruit. Eat it quick or it will spoil."

"Eat me slowly."

"I've been smoking."

"Is that why you want me so?"

"I wanted you the moment that I saw you."

"So you really are a whore?"

"Does it really make a difference?"

"Can you see me? I can see you. You are so exquisite."

I come upon her cottage as I round a bend: two unpainted turrets made of mud bricks set some thirty feet apart connected by a wooden footbridge on the second floor. The roof is conical and made of thatch. On the side of either turret there are simple shutters held aloft with driftwood set in grooves along the sills.

"Where are you?" I say into the phone.

"In the front."

"But I am there."

"No. You're in the back. Follow your nose."

I take a leaf-strewn path through ferns and bougainvillea and there before me on a wooden bench suspended from an afroed mango tree is Frances Carey.

Her sleeveless dress is white with cream embroidery. The neck is square. There are buttons in the front. Some of them are loose. One leg is dangling. One knee is drawn up; there she rests her elbow.

I watch the fabric pooling in the space between her thighs. I can feel the way it tickles all the hairs I cannot see from thirty yards away. The leaves are sifting light across her bosom, dusting her as one would drizzle sugar on a warm confection.

"And what now?" I ask, slipping the phone into my pocket.

"Just stand there let me look at you?"

I extend my arms and make a joke of slowly turning round.

"Is that all for me?" she asks. She lifts her other heel against the bench.

As I walk toward her crickets leap out from the tufted grass.

Twenty yards away I stop again.

With a twist she pulls a button. Twists again and loosens two. She pulls a strap across her shoulder. But before the strap descends along her arm she stops.

Below her collarbone I see the way her flesh begins to gather force, preparing to erupt in waves of breasts.

"You are so fucking bad," I say. "I can't believe I ever thought that you were lovely and charming."

"I have changed my mind. You are not at all exquisite. You are such an ugly boy. What I am going to do with you? The ugly ones are always best, though. They always want to hide their face inside your crotch."

She braces on her heels and flashes out her dress. I glimpse damp thigh and black panties. She brings her knees together and the hem now shrouds her ankles and her instep, almost to her toes.

I am close enough to touch her now. The sun is falling low

behind me. To look into my face she has to lean away and shade her eyes. She has to squint to focus.

She shakes her head and bites her lip. Perhaps she is feeling something deep inside her. Perhaps she understands that from my vantage point her act looks like a cower. Perhaps now that I'm close to her, close enough for her to see my bobbing Adam's apple, close enough for her to smell the hormones in my sweat, close enough for her to hear my breathing, she has had a revelation—that I've recovered from the spell of her charisma, that there is something quaintly ritualistic in the whiteness of her clothes, that she is the dove who brushed the whiskers of the lazy cat.

She holds my gaze. Her lips begin to quiver. She looks away as if she is trying to recollect the rules. When she looks again she sees a face that says that there are rules but that I've bribed the referee.

"I had a vibe about you," she whispers. She takes my hands and brings them to her shoulders. "A *very* strong vibe about you."

"Is that right?"

"But you know this."

For a moment we are still, and then the lovely and charming Frances Carey, who was born in Guyana on February 11, 1963, and came to live in Jamaica with her father in 1981, at the age of seventeen, after a cataclysmic argument with her mother, reaches up to kiss me.

Her tongue is small, but it isn't shy. Neither are her hands. And as our kisses become more desperate, and our clinking teeth announce the loss of concentration, she insinuates her palms beneath my shirt and finds the grooves between the muscles that embank my spine.

Her knees are pressed together. She is sitting on her dress. The bench begins to swing. I hold the rope to steady it and touch her through the cloth.

Her thighs are solid but they're creamed with what Jamaicans know as glam, the foamy fat that jiggles when a woman walks, the mud that hides the wattles of her bones.

Not cellulite. Glam. Cellulite is flung against a body from a distance. Glam is fat smoothed on by God with patience . . . a smear against the hamstring . . . a smudge along the crescent where the bottom meets the thigh . . . a daub below the navel . . . a spackle on the flanks . . . sometimes thick, but always clear enough to show the effort of the muscles underneath . . . each twist . . . each jerk . . . each tension and release.

"At first I was afraid that this would happen," Frances moans.

"This what?"

"This *this*. This what's happening now."

She reaches up and tears my shirt and laughs. Craning now, she takes my nipple in her mouth. Her face is now a fist inscribing with a calligraphic pen. She draws words on my chest, traces curlicues and serifs and other flourishes.

Laughing too, I rip her dress. Her legs erupt like birds astonished by a shot. The cloth collapses in a pool around her pelvis. Her calves embrace me. Her ankles tie a knot behind my back. I release the rope and grip the handles. She begins to swing away from me. My shoes begin to drag.

She reaches down between my legs.

"It is so fat. It is too fat. Too big and fucking fat. I can't do this. No, I can't. No, I can't. It will never fit inside me. How will you fit this beast inside me?"

When I pause to reassure her, to calm her down, I notice that she is smiling from the corner of her mouth. This is a play.

By now my wood is iron. So hard it is unfeeling. I cannot tell if I am in or out. I close my eyes and concentrate. I think I sense a fabric. Mine or hers? Underwear? Whose underwear? Silk or cotton? Boxers or a thong?

As I think of this I feel her lean away from me. And burned into my retina is the image of Frances Carey as she drapes her dress across her face, making it a veil.

She brings her knees up to her shoulders, sinks her heels into my chest, reaches down between her legs and finger-rips her panty-crotch.

"Don't wait now, Carey. Kill it."

And I plunge, sawing at the ropes that keep her love from coming down.

"I feel it," she moans.

"Bring it," I whisper.

"I feel it. My God."

"Come, sweet girl, I'll hold you."

"You have a gift for me?"

"Yes, baby."

"And you wrapping it up for me?"

"Yes, darling."

"Tying it up with ribbons?"

"Yes, lover."

"Adding a bow?"

"Do you know who you are? You're my conqueror."

"And you're bringing it for me?"

"Only my man can make me come like this, so fast, you know."

"So there you go."

"What? Where? Who goes? Are you my man?"

"You want me to be your man, right now?"

"You want me to come?"

"But of course."

"You want me to come and scream your name so Poonks and Papa Bear can hear us?"

"That's my greatest wish."

"So tell me you're my man then?"

"Okay, then. I am your man."

"Are you my man?"

"I am your man. I am your negro. I'm your master. I'm your boss."

"So here ... here ... take the pussy then ... do what you want with it. You own it, Daddy. Do anything you want. Even sell it."

● CHAPTER NINE

"What are you thinking?"

We are in her room. I am sitting with my back against the headboard, legs extended, ankles crossed, cradling her head in my lap, blowing streams of air against her temples.

"What are you thinking?" she repeats.

I close my eyes and laugh, for I am thinking that in theory I could die tomorrow, for I've made love to the woman I would sleep with on my final night on earth.

"At Rozette's you said that you're the kind of man who reads a woman poems in the happy ever after. A man must keep his word."

I rock her as she chuckles. Outside, it has begun to rain. I recite some lines of verse from Nicolas Guillén. When I'm through she's curled up tightly, rubbing her face on my stomach.

"Thank you very much," she says.

"You are very welcome, love."

"And make sure to lock the door behind you when you leave. The latch is kind of funny."

I gather that I must have tried to stutter a reply.

"Oh, what?" she asks.

My fingers seek a spot of weakness in the sheets. I begin to pick the threading with my nails. I have an urgent need to rip or shred or bore.

What is she trying to do? Does she even know what she has done? How could she be so blasé with my feelings?

"What?" she emphasizes.

"Nothing," I reply.

"What is it?" She rubs her eyes. "Seriously."

Looking askance I say to her: "I . . . thought I heard you telling me to close the door behind me."

"That is what I said," she answers, daring me with nonchalance. The poison from her words is seeping through my arteries, seizing all my muscles, bringing me down. "But I was joking."

She begins to punch me in the stomach as she laughs, slaps my face as if she needs to bring me back to life.

What is there to do but laugh as well?

"Come fall asleep with me," she offers, lying on her side. As she lies there I begin to kiss her feet, rubbing my cheeks against her calves.

The prickles on her shin and the poem by Guillén elicit a remembrance of Cuba, of riding tractors through the canefields, arms extended, the brush of leaves against my fingers, the stalks majestic in the rags of their own dried trash like the Africans whose blood-waters fed that soil.

Riding on the tractor I used to feel a scent mist up inside me, a scent like something offered up in flames. Frances, this scent is gummed around your follicles.

I slide up and lie beside her, slip my leg across her thigh and take a raisin-colored nipple in my mouth.

"Come here, baby darling," she whispers. "Come for some bubby. Oh, you are in need of so much sonning. I can tell that your mother didn't love you up when you were small. Come, baby darling. Come, come. Drink up. I am your mother now. Mummy has condensed milk and brown sugar in the bubby. Take all you want, my son. Who is your mother, big man?"

"You, Mummy."

"Tell me again."

"Only you."

CHAPTER TEN

Something terrible has happened. What, I am not sure. But I have awakened on my back and Frances has her knees on either side of me.

Her overlapping hands are clamped across her mouth. She is peering through her fingers.

It is night. The room is dark. How long have I been sleeping?

"Are you okay?"

We say this at the same time but in different voices.

She shuts her eyes and lifts her head, allows her hands to fall. I ease up on my elbows. She falls on me . . . begins to cry, her muscles stiff, her skin now cold with perspiration.

"Did you have a bad dream?" I whisper. She is not holding me. She is clutching herself, holding something inside.

"Did you have a bad dream?" I ask again. "Everybody has bad dreams, baby. Sometimes I have them, too."

"I know," she says. "I know. You just had one. You were thrashing and crying. When I tried to calm you down you hit me."

Something falls inside me. A muscle near my belly button clenches like a fist to hold it.

"Carey, is there something that you need to say?"

"Frances, I am sorry."

"Not like that. Something deeper, more important?"

A segment of the moon begins to float across the window. I use it to distract her and we watch the sky in stillness until she is animated by a thought.

"Make love to me," she whispers. "Don't fuck me like you did before. If I'm sounding quite entitled then forgive me. I just need that right now—from you." I begin to speak but she palms my mouth. "If you don't know what to do then do nothing. Just feel me. Just look at me. Just experience me. Don't think about anything or anyone but me. Is that too much to ask?"

"No, it isn't."

She senses my discomfort, my sense that this is leading me to places where I might not want to go.

"Be big about it," she challenges. "Take it like a man. Any little boy can fuck a woman. Boys rehearse fucking in the bathroom with a jar of Vaseline when they are twelve years old. Making love is a whole other thing. Making love is all about surrender, about opening up and admitting things inside you. Girls have to learn to fuck. Boys are born that way. Make love to me, Carey. You can do it. I will teach you. I will show you how to open up yourself and feel me way down deep inside you."

I begin to protest but she cuts me off: "Follow me and you will get the fuck of your life."

She rolls away from me. On either nightstand is a votive in an alabaster cup. She lights one and then the other. The stone begins to glow.

She reaches past my head toward the wall, her navel pressing on my nose. There is the sound of effort, of things unraveling, of cordage and a winch, then white mosquito netting splashes down. Now we are cocooned. And with this shelter comes a different mood.

The moon, the net, the golden light, they soften me. Her kisses soak into my skin. Her touches leave impressions.

Her lips begin to brush my lashes.

"Close your eyes."

I obey. She positions my body in a cross, then straddles me on hands and knees.

"Now focus on my heat," she whispers. "Think of nothing else."

At first there is nothing. I knit my brows. She tells me to inhale and hold it. When my cheeks begin to tremble Frances signals me to let it out, and something rushes in against the tide.

"That's it," she says, "now hold it. I have given you my heat. Now you have me with you for all time. From now on all you have to do is think of me to warm yourself. Breathe deeply."

Something hard begins to melt inside me.

"Didn't I tell you that you needed some release?" she asks. "A lot of things are binding you. Love will set you free."

From the melting thing inside me comes two streams. One courses down my belly then divides at my erection, flowing through my legs into my toes. The other seeps along my breastbone to my collarbone, where it splashes through my arms into my fingers. I feel a pulsing at the tips of my extremities, then the streams begin to filter through my pores into the sheets. I begin to feel as if I am floating in warm water. And I realize that the melting thing is memory.

"You are floating," she says. "In the distance is a waterfall. Don't be afraid to tumble over."

I hear someone calling my name.

"Now you have my heat in you. Now focus on my sound."

I pull it through the clackering of the insects and the rustling of the trees and the thudding of the blood against my temples. It is the rasping of our pubic hairs.

"Hold that sound," she urges. "Don't lose it."

As I focus on the sound I feel her head against my shoulder, against my ribs the hardness of her nipples then the softness of her breasts.

She spreads my ankles with her toes, creates her space between my legs then takes me deep inside her.

"Focus on the sound," she tells me. "Don't focus on what you're feeling."

She brings my knees toward my chest and whispers, "I am elemental now. Just sound. I have no form. Neither do you. Just sound. Just air. Just essence. Now we can travel where we need to go. Take me to your dreams, sweet boy. Take me to your dreams."

A haze begins to seep across my vision. Highlights float and glimmer in the dark. I try to raise myself but feel as if my bones are fixed.

"Carey, you are trying to escape yourself."

"Jesus Christ, I cannot move."

"Of course you can't. You are coming."

I wrench myself and for a second I erupt out of my body, and from this vantage point I gain a peek across the cataracts of memory, and see into another world, returning to my body with the substance of the dream.

"I saw you before I met you," Frances whispers as we lie together, holding hands. "You didn't come clear-clear like how you are now. I don't know if you remember at Rozette's the way I shook my head when I found out you are a writer?" She pauses. "Can I ask you something? Do you feel something special for me, Carey? And I'm not asking you this question as some innocent girl who has screwed a guy to build her self-esteem or something. I am a woman of experience. I simply want to know."

I squeeze her hand.

"I am sorry, Frances. But I really cannot talk right now."

"Do you know why I slept with you like that?" she presses. "Without really knowing you?"

I turn my head away.

"Can we talk about this later?"

"You are so frustrating!"

She rolls across the bed and leaves the room.

I find her on the footbridge, leaning on the banister. She winces when she hears me, her shoulder blades flashing through her skin like hatchets. I stand behind her, willing her to turn around. I do not know her well enough to know what will assuage her.

"Frances I am sorry for frustrating you."

"Oh, fuck off."

"You are not allowed to talk to me like that."

"You're not my man," she sneers, glancing back. "We were just pretending. I talk to you the way I talk to anyone."

"Do you know what? I'm leaving. I should have closed the door behind me long ago."

"No, wait."

She takes my hand. We go inside.

Now that we have argued we have history. Without fighting, everything between a couple is just experience. History is the narrative of wars.

"We have to talk," she tells me as she holds my face. "We have to talk about your dream."

"What do you mean?"

"*Mulewe anekoso kuduwe bana.*"

I have had a recurring dream since I was twelve years old. It comes to me perhaps ten times a year. I have not been able to remember it clearly until now. The setting is West Africa. A boy I know to be myself is sheltering with a girl beside a boulder near the rapids of a stream. They have run away.

It is raining. They are weak. And they are whispering in a language that I sense but do not understand. They do not know what they should do. Keep running or go back? Where is there to go? What lies across the river? The unknown.

With gathered fruit inside a gourd they make an offering to the ancestors; then they wade into the stream. The rushing water rises higher, to their shoulders, past their necks. Then as they take their final breath and plunge into the current they are found and captured . . . the hunting party comes . . . men with spears and bows, at times a rusty harquebus.

The children flail and thrash. Their tribesmen drag them out, curse them, beat them, chain their limbs. The boy is forced to walk. The girl is shoved inside an iron cage constructed on a litter.

"*Mulewe anekoso kuduwe bana,*" she shouts before they gag her. The young boy cries the same.

I have never said this phrase aloud. I've never written it down. And I've never cared about its meaning until now.

"Carey," Frances asks me. "Do you know what '*Mulewe anekoso kuduwe bana*' means?"

"No. I don't."

"Carey, you were speaking Hora," she declares expectantly. "That's my native language."

I am picking at the sheet. I pause before I answer.

"But Frances, you are Guyanese."

"What gave you that idea? I am from Ghana."

In the rain I did not hear Rozette correctly. Or perhaps this is a joke.

"My grandfather was Ghanaian," I offer emptily.

"If so, then so are you. Where was he from?"

"I don't know. He didn't know. He was an orphan."

"But you are not," she tells me. "I'm your mother."

She pulls me to the floor. The tiles are cool against my skin.

"Let me tell you something, Carey. It doesn't really matter if you believe me. Tell you what, let's take it as a joke. You will end up doing what you want anyway."

"And what is that?"

There is a bit of sharpness in my voice. At times I find her wisdom quite invasive.

"And what is what?"

"And what will I want to do?"

She runs her thumb across my brow.

"Oh, you will want to stay with me."

What gives her the right to be this way, so contrary and immodest? I gaze into her eyes. She does not flinch. I blink away a memory, and she laughs and says, "I win."

This is what Everton's grandmother had to say to me: *You are about to meet your match.*

The Horas are concentrated in the north," Frances tells me as we shower. I have just told her that I have never heard about them. "Near the border with Burkina Faso."

She is scrubbing my back with a loofah. If history for me is defined by war, history for her is defined by blood. My heritage has brought out the sweetness in her. She is no longer the trickster, the woman who needs to tease and hurt.

"So you are from the north?" I ask.

"My family. I was born in Accra."

"I was born in New York."

"You have a Hora name, you know. Your name is Karamoko."

"Why that and not something else like Anthony or Bruce?"

"Oh, the legend of Karamoko."

"I am a legend in my own time? That's very cool."

"Oh, shut it."

"Okay, then tell me."

"You have to turn around.

"Karamoko was a boy who was sold into slavery at the age

of twelve as punishment for eloping with the daughter of the Hora king. The Hora are not Akan people like the Ashanti. We have different customs and beliefs. And although we hardly intermarry we have lived in peace for most of history. The trouble with the Ashanti started when the Asantehene, the king of the Ashanti, wanted to marry Feranje, the daughter of the Hora king. When the Hora king said no, the Asantehene gave an ultimatum: If the princess was not sent to him in peace, he would send his army to kidnap her and she would live forever as his concubine. But Feranje was in love with Karamoko, the son of the chief of the royal guard, and when she heard the news that her father had promised her to the Asantehene, she and Karamoko ran away. They were caught, Karamoko was sold into slavery and Feranje was taken to the Asantehene. When Karamoko and Feranje were captured they screamed to each other, '*Mulewe anekoso kuduwe bana.*' That means, 'I will search until I find you.' And ever since their separation, Karamoko and Feranje have been searching for each other in successive lives."

We go to bed and lie waiting for the sun to rise, our fingers whispering poems in the language of our skins, free verse punctuated with loose promises.

"Can I tell you something, Carey?" I squeeze her just above the elbow. "I know that I am Feranje."

"That is neither here nor there," I tell her. "I am here for my own reasons."

"Ever since I was a little girl I have been dreaming this dream about running away with this young boy and being captured and married off to this old man. I didn't understand it till I was maybe twenty-five. That is when I read about the legend of Karamoko and Feranje."

"We have a connection, Frances . . . but it is something very different."

"You are American, but you understand my language?"

It would be hard to contradict her without seeming conde-scending.

"A line is not a whole language, Frances. Don't take that the wrong way."

"*Ganga nin tudubai namgal erendeh. Nupqal latimab sine gussu entebge ndenti obrassa settu uggu?*"

"Come on Frances, you must admit that meeting a reincar-nated lover isn't an everyday experience. I think there is enough of you for me to love in this life. I don't need another one."

"So how did you understand what I just said to you?"

I roll away from her, trying to find a space to reconvene myself. Stripped of my defenses, I've abandoned me.

"You've had the same dream, haven't you, Carey?"

"I don't want to talk about it."

She presses.

"Haven't you?"

"How did you know?"

"So you understand my language and we have the same re-curring dream? What will it take for you to believe?"

To understand my feelings, Frances, you will have to under-stand my God . . . the God who gave me life and who will not hesitate to take it away, the vengeful Jah of the Old Testament, the one who turned the Nile into a river of blood, and plagued Egypt with frogs, and turned its dust to maggots, and swarmed its homes with flies, and struck down its cows with pestilence, and infested its people with boils, and flattened its landscape with hail, and withered its fields with locusts, and dimmed the light of its sun, and killed its firstborn children with speed and no remorse.

My God is a jealous God. A God of retribution. He demands complete allegiance. He will not be mocked or forsaken. He punctuates his thoughts with natural forces: A gale is a comma, rain is an ellipsis . . . a thunder ball a period. And lightning is a dramatic exclamation point!

And I tested him severely when I tried to kill myself. I am cherishing this second chance.

"Carey," Frances interrupts. "Come with me to Kingston in the morning."

"You don't have a car and I have to catch a plane."

"They are bringing me another one."

"Okay."

"So fuck the flight," she urges, tickling my ribs.

"Oh no. Fuck you."

"That's a great idea. Come to Kingston in the morning and fuck me."

CHAPTER ELEVEN

Moved by an odd nostalgia, I leave postcards at the front desk before I go—one to my brother, a plastic surgeon in Las Vegas; another to my mother, who now lives in Tel Aviv; and for my sisters, both of whom are teachers in Toronto, I dispatch by express mail two pounds of high mountain coffee beans and some reggae CDs chosen from the offerings in the gift shop. After this I say good-bye to Everton, Poonks, and Papa Bear, and loiter in the parking lot for Frances.

Her second car, the one that was brought from Kingston, is an Alfa Romeo, a Duetto Spider convertible, a strap-on dildo in the grip of a woman who drives in the same way she loves. Zestfully. Daringly. Recklessly. And skilled.

Leaning back in the tall black seat, a red scarf tied around her hair, she drives with one hand on the wheel, the other on my thigh. Wedged between her legs is a bottle of spring water that tightens her *lappa*, which is red and yellow and edged with fringes tipped with glass buttons, creating waves of folds that ray down from her center to her open knees.

Beyond Port Antonio, the land begins to heave and fall along the foothills of tall mountains, and Frances calmly points the speeding silver car along the road, which is thin and curly and hems to the sea like a line of black embroidery.

We are dropping down a slope into St. Margaret's Bay, and the wind is coming off the sea up through the moss-draped trees as we take the iron bridge across the Rio Grande. Down below and to the right is Rafter's Rest, where I first saw her in the flesh.

We have been talking animatedly along the way, engaging in a free-form conversation. I have been mostly listening.

Like a pelican skimming across the waves her voice is low and fast above the engine, which crests and falls with the shifting gears. She has spoken of the tragedy of Fela Kuti, of the evil of the IMF, of the joys of river bathing, of the economic possibilities of converting all the island's canefields into wind farms, acres and acres of windmills that would generate enough electric power to drive a strong economy. We then begin to talk about the yoke of independence, of how hard it is for former colonies to make it in the world, and she says that independence "is just fucking overrated. I want my man to rule me."

She says this with defiance, a defiance that is almost sympathetic, for she knows that ruling her is not an easy task. At heart she is a rebel, and rebels understand the burden of rule. And that is why they do not want to govern. They simply want the government to listen to their wishes. So they fight to get attention. Frances is a rebel. She is not a revolutionary. She doesn't want to overturn the way that men relate to women; she just wants intelligent rule. This intrigues and frightens me. Do I have what it takes to make her happy?

"Is ruling you the only perk that comes with being your man?" I tease.

On either side of us are fields of wild ginger.

"No," she replies. "My man will get a lot of perks. If he rules me right I will pay my taxes—fuck him and feed him and spoil him to death."

"And what would be the role of government in this republic?"

She ignores the abstract nature of my question and answers it concretely.

"You have to love me and respect me, but more than that you must inspire me. Be vulnerable and funny, and make me know that when it comes down to it you'll defend me with your life."

"So I wouldn't have to fuck you and feed you and spoil you as well?"

"But that goes without saying."

"And that's it?"

"There are other things. But I prefer to keep them close to the vest."

She says this with a coyness that is actually a challenge, daring me to pry the information out of her while denying to myself that there is something blazingly erotic in fulfilling a desire with the able use of force.

"The breast?" I joke.

"No," she says. "The vest."

I feign weak hearing.

"The breast."

"Okay. If that is what you need to hear—the breast."

I reach. She pats my hand and looks at me with playful eyes. I place the other hand on her shoulder. Without looking, she removes it, commanding me to stop. I negotiate a feel . . . a touch . . . a brush with the back of my hand. She resists and this inflames me.

"What is all of this?" I ask. A crosswind pulls my shirt across my nipples. "I just need to touch you."

"Not now."

Her voice is firm but friendly.

"If not now, then when?"

"Maybe later."

"Why then and not now?"

"I don't need a reason. . . . They're mine."

"Just a touch . . . just one touch . . . just one breast."

I raise a finger.

"Which one?"

"The left one."

"Why that one?"

"Because it's closest to me."

"Emotionally?"

"Oh, stop."

"So, Mr. McCullough wants to touch Miss Carey's breast."

She resettles herself in her seat.

"Yes, Miss Carey . . . badly."

"Show me your dick and I'll consider it."

She looks at me then at the road again. We are in a line of swiftly moving traffic now. A truck is right behind us.

"Of course you're joking."

"This is not a game. Fork it out."

I glance over my shoulder.

"And do what?"

"I am undecided. But something interesting. Maybe you could kneel on your seat and I could suck you as I drive. You would have to be my eyes and tell me how to steer."

"You are sick."

"And so are you, because you are considering it."

Road construction brings the conversation to a halt. We have stopped in the middle of a little town and the musty masculinity of the laborers infuses me with new resolve.

"I can't take my dick out just like that," I tell her as we begin to move again.

We are arcing in a falling curve between the forest and the sea.

She pats my leg.

"And that is good. If you did I think I would've been a little disappointed."

"Why?"

"Because it would mean that I could rule you."

I look at her. She looks at me. I hold her stare. She bites her lip. I lift her hand away from me.

"Frances Carey, show me your fucking breasts."

She undoes the knot and the shirt falls open. She slips a finger from her chin along her throat, unknots the scarf, stuffs it in the mouth of the water bottle that she holds between her legs, then looks toward me for approval. I raise a brow. As I watch her now, she slips the blouse off one shoulder, for a moment releases the steering wheel, removes the other side, then, holding the wheel with one hand now, hooks the blouse on her index finger and raises her arm in the wind, which sweeps it with a flutter like a sheet of old newspaper. As her breasts begin to shimmer with the roughness of the road I unknot my hair and throw my shirt like caution to the wind.

The sea is gurgling. The sun smiles hard. Natty dread rides again.

But as we zephyr past an old stone church, I face the realization that I am doing something wrong, and I withdraw into an uninviting silence.

I should be going to South Carolina. Instead I'm on part two of the magical mystery tour in a speeding car being driven by a topless African who believes that I am her reincarnated lover.

A part of me understands this as a craving for adventure. But another part of me believes that I'm in love.

This doesn't worry me because I fall out of love as easily as I fall in. An ex of mine once told me that I have never been in love and will never be. Love, I tried to explain to her, is like weather—not climate. Today's cold front does not erase last Monday's ninety-nine degrees.

As we drive along in silence, I begin to think of Frances as a guest on an episode of *Trapped in Transit*—a few episodes actually—paired on each segment with a different one of my exes.

At first the idea is grudgingly amusing. But it soon becomes foreboding as I listen in my head to all the things that they might share—awful things, nasty things, a lot of them, honestly, true.

I would be very disappointed if Frances heard these things. For I am not the man I used to be. What would I do if she heard these things and told me that she could not see me anymore? I would be upset. No, sad. Devastated, I am beginning to believe.

There is a woman by the name of Sarah Walters who, I suppose, would love to speak with Frances. There is little chance that this will happen. I have neither seen nor heard from her in years, although I occupy the house in which we lived.

Like Pa McCullough, I went to Cambridge, but I wasn't bright enough to be a doctor, so I took my chance with English. I did badly in my first year and transferred to Sussex. I had ambitions for a Ph.D., and the endurance for a master's. Sometimes I think I must have bribed someone for my degree because I don't remember doing any work. Most of my time was spent in the theater or at the home of Charles Gillespie, the noted Irish dramaturge, who by then was well into his eighties and had directed Gielgud and Burton and his favorite, Richard Harris.

In 1984, on Gillespie's recommendation, I was hired on to the faculty of NYU. Up until this point, only one of my plays had been staged in America, *La Isla Negra*, an absurdist evocation of an affair between Pablo Neruda and Gwendolyn Brooks. But three of my plays had been produced at the Royal Court in London, and most importantly, I had directed a production of *The Seagull* for the BBC.

La Isla Negra was panned by the *New York Times*. And in retrospect, it should have been. But the reviewer for the *Village Voice*, Sarah Walters, described it as "a masterwork provoked to mischief by a deviant mind." And by the time of my arrival she and I had carried on a six-month correspondence.

When we met in person, I discovered very early that I had made a serious error. Sarah was not as smart as I had thought. What she was was clever. Her mind was a sort of Kelvinator, a fridge in which she kept the bottled theories she had picked up out of clever books, theories she would drizzle over wilting leaves of prose like store-bought salad dressing.

Sarah was the center of a group of negro writers at the *Voice*. Like me they were young, self-referential, and conceited. Having lived outside the States for years I had a neutral accent, but on returning to New York I decided to be English. I was determined to stand out.

To Sarah and her friends I was quite impressive—a British-educated, Rastafarian Jew who had lived in Cuba. To me they were impressionable. They wore their boho hipness with the self-assurance of a clan of country cousins dressed in borrowed suits. Black for them was boring. In their eyes "the movement" had failed. Unity meant failure. They were determined to be different. And I represented so much of what that difference could be.

And so I became more self-absorbed. And when I noticed that Sarah had begun to paraphrase me in her writing, I began to toss off bits of rubbish with a calculated nonchalance, then wait a week to see it printed: "The new feminism will be the post-postmodern world's riposte to the screech of postindustrial angst."

On the day that she was promoted to a columnist, Sarah told me that she thought she was in love. We were walking down Fifth Avenue and had just crossed over Eighth Street, fording a stream of young shoe shoppers, and I turned to look at her, tall and anorexic, with a shaven head, an upturned nose, and cheeks made rough by acne.

"In love?" I asked. "In love with whom?"

She told me as we passed beneath the Roman arch in Washington Square.

"With you."

"And why is this?"

She removed her shades and held my hand. Young West Indian herbalists were playing soccer near the fountain, ignoring the comedian who was setting up his little amp and tapping on his microphone.

"Because it is so hard to find a negro who *really* understands the deeper meaning of the Fine Young Cannibals."

I went along for the adventure.

Sarah was a feminist, a graduate of Brown who introduced me to cocaine and Rita Dove.

Like many columnists, at the *Voice* and other places, Sarah really wrote about herself. She thought that she was ugly. The truth is that she was. And I can say this with such honesty because I secretly believe that she made herself that way in service to her art.

I have seen the pictures. She used to be lovely, broad-hipped and high-breasted, the puggish nose an accent in a face whose lines were as romantic as a ballad: long cheekbones, frilly lips, skin the sweat-tempered golden brown of trumpets.

Sarah understood the need for columnists to have a territory, a claim, something that can justify their sense of self-importance, something worthy of fixation. The world winces when a child murmurs that she is ugly. When a woman says it, though, we want to cry.

For the early part of our relationship I lived in an apartment on Washington Square and she lived in Chinatown.

One winter in her apartment, as I creamed her ribs and abdomen with olive oil and shea butter, Sarah told me that some friends of hers had found us an apartment, an abandoned house in Brooklyn. To this point we had made no plans to live together.

"Downstairs would be the performance space," she said excitedly, "and we could occupy the floors above."

"I am not sure about that," I replied.

"What do you mean? We have to take those buildings back."

"Take them back? We never owned them."

"There will come a time," she said, "when you will come into a fuller understanding of the imperatives of class struggle and revolution."

Her father was a judge. Her mother was an orthodontist. Her great-grandparents had a home on Martha's Vineyard. I looked at her and shook my head and laughed.

"Why are you so obsessed with being underground?" I asked. "With living on the margins? Black people in Africa are occupying the center of their societies. Where is the common sense and honor in living on the margins in the places where we were enslaved?"

The idea was absurd, but I agreed, and for two years we lived together in a single room of what used to be a rooming house on Clermont Avenue. We had neither heat nor hot water.

In the mornings I would ride my black Ducati to my classes. She would stay at home, do coke, write, and supervise the renovations, which in essence meant she would offer me her latest great idea in the evenings, along with rough sketches of grand plans as I sat glumly near the plug-in radiator, a sheaf of student scripts in hand, wondering what had happened to my life. Why had I moved from Greenwich Village to a street where old brownstones with chipped facades were interspersed with empty lots, a street that called to mind a smile with broken dentures?

There was a park across the street, and at night, from my window on the highest floor, I would see young women leading men beyond the jungle gym, beyond the radius of the streetlights, into wading pools of darkness.

One fall evening I arrived at home to find the moldy, broken staircase strewn with white gardenias.

Sarah was sitting on the edge of the bed in black jeans, leaning back on her elbows, topless, the fly of her jeans undone, as if she had consumed a heavy meal.

"There is news," she said as I entered. "I did the math. I think we should buy this house. I tracked down the owner. It's the city. It has a lot of violations, but we could get it for a hundred thousand dollars."

"That's interesting," I said absently. On the table by the bed there was a mirror dusted with white powder.

"Things are different now." She placed her hand on her stomach. "We're having a child."

I pointed to the mirror and the coke.

"No, Sarah. *We* are not."

By then I had already lost eight children.

We had an argument. Not about cocaine and pregnancy as one would think. We had an argument about freedom and control.

From there on Sarah's writing changed. She stopped writing about herself—and began to write about me, the man who made her pregnant to control her. It was the autumn of the patriarch.

Still I bought the house. Still I put her name on the deed— because she was my woman, pregnant with my child, and moving there had been her idea. And still she exposed our most private conversations, our most fragile moments, our coldest whispers, our most incandescent arguments to the world. Eventually I stopped speaking. Eventually I stopped coming home. I began to have affairs . . . well, more of them. In fact I was in Venezuela with another woman when Sarah went for her abortion. I had left her money and a note:

Do what you have to do. As your readers might have guessed, I think we might be done.

To indulge herself, or perhaps it was to spite me, Sarah underwent the operation with just local anesthesia—so she would be clear to take notes, interview the doctor, and write a cover story for the *Voice* about the process. The liquefaction of my child was news.

I had to leave New York. I rode my motorcycle to a job in Minnesota at St. Regis College; there, I met Kwabena.

CHAPTER TWELVE

About a mile outside Annotto Bay, Frances makes a turn along a gravel road and we proceed through dense rain forest. Light sprays down in dusty shafts, striping the leaves in the under-growth.

The trees suspire in the glaring brightness of an open meadow that ends in a cliff, and we park in the shadow of a crumbled house and pick our way through cow dung and wildflowers to a windswept tree that overlooks the water. There we collapse in the arms of the welcoming shade and roll two spliffs in silence, gazing at the taut mouth of the horizon, which exhales its scudding waves toward the shore.

Frances's body is soft against me, but I sense in its quiescence a murmuring, a whispering of questions, a tense but civil debate.

She lays her head in my lap and I massage her scalp, coaxing the words from her. Matches. They're in the car. We retrace our steps through the grass.

"So who are you?" she asks, as we smoke on the hood of the Alfa. "Rozette has told me a couple of things, but I want to hear from you."

"What did she say?"

"Well, for one," she begins, "I heard you were the most troublesome boy in the history of your high school—always getting detentions for lateness and wisecracking and chatting too much in class."

"Yeah, that's true. I was the class clown. But I wasn't that bad."

"I also heard you were a soccer star. Do you still play?"

I reach into the car for a paper bag, ball it in my hands, and juggle it from knee to knee.

"Do I still play? I don't know. You tell me."

"You are such a little show-off."

"So what else did Rozette tell you?"

I kick the ball in the air and catch it.

"That you sing a bit and play a little guitar."

"A little bit."

I reach between her thighs for the water.

"Do you feel complete?" she asks.

"What do you mean?"

"Is there anything missing from your life, anything you want to do or achieve before you pass on?"

"Before I die? Write a play that's a quarter as good as *Death and the King's Horseman*, have some children, and become the benevolent dictator of a country populated with naked women who look exactly like you."

She leans her head and looks at me. As I smile at her she looks away toward the sea and starts to hum, which brings me once again into the memory of the first time that I saw her, that time when I was ready to surrender my life, and my thoughts turn again to dying.

"Frances," I ask, "here is a scenario. On the night before you go to the gallows you're given the chance to eat a last meal, make love to one person, hear one last song, read one last book, and have your meal with any writer—living or dead."

She thinks about it briefly then replies.

"I would read my diaries. I'm sure they'd be more accurate than whatever montage my brain would flash before my eyes. My last meal would be something Ghanaian, something like *gari* with groundnut stew and maybe a little pepper soup."

"What about the last song?"

"I'm not sure. Maybe something by Fela, or maybe something by Jimi Hendrix, a blues, something like 'Hear My Train A Coming.' But I'm not sure if I'd pick the acoustic or the electric version."

"And who would you have for dinner?"

"The person has to be a writer?"

She fidgets as she smiles, animated by the excitement of choice.

"Maryse Condé, maybe." She pauses and begins to pout. "Or more likely, Kofi Awoonor."

"And the last person you would sleep with?"

She smiles and looks away.

"I don't know what to say."

A muscle twitches in my chest.

"Just say what you feel like saying."

"But that is the kind of thing a person needs to think about."

Soon I will be tedious. I know this. But I cannot help myself.

"Okay, is it just a fuck or something meaningful?" she asks.

I want to turn and walk away. I do not trust that I can keep my sentiments from showing on my face.

I am jealous. Not just now. Jealousy is a condition. When I love a woman I want to be more than her man. I want to be her child—possess her full attention, be loved unconditionally, nurtured, and spoilt. But I'll never say it. I will *will* it though. And hope for it. And maneuver and manipulate to achieve it. But I'll never request it. Because it is unreasonable.

Just a fuck?

In the millisecond it takes to blink away a glare, I see projected on the lining of my eyelids a pornographic documentary on her life. I see men I do not know; men I *know* she does not know; men I know and begin to wonder *if* she knows; African men, Jamaican men, dirty old men, athletes, musicians, fat bankers in their weekend whites; cane cutters with rough hands; gangsters, deacons, movie stars; her father's trusted friends.

Which one is she considering? Which sweet, slow grind is stirring up her belly . . . fertilizing her desires? Which jook against the side of a house? Whose cum is clogging up her larynx . . . throttling all responses but a moan?

I want to know . . . and then again, I don't.

Just a fuck?

The word *fuck* bothers me. It seems crass for what I want to be a sentimental moment. I don't want my Frances to be fucking on her last night on earth. I want her to have a final bond with a significant love. Why? Because fucking reduces my importance to her, because she's fucked more men than she's loved, and she's the woman I would sleep with on my final night on earth. No, she should not fuck. She should have a final bond with a significant love and that person should be me.

"If it's just a fuck," she begins, "I'd take—"

"What time is it?" I interrupt.

"Almost noon."

"I guess I won't be making that flight."

"I didn't know that you still had that intention."

"Well, it doesn't matter now. I just need to make a couple of phone calls."

"Are you hungry?" she asks.

"I guess I am."

She takes my hand.

"So let's go then."

I need some time away from her.

"Why don't you go and get us something? We could have a picnic here."

"I'll find whatever you want."

"I'll eat whatever you bring."

● CHAPTER THIRTEEN

I telephone Kwabena as she leaves. Nazia answers the phone.

"Maybe you should speak with him yourself," she tells me when she gets the news. I have missed the plane. At best I'll be arriving tomorrow.

"Do you want to talk to him?" she prompts.

"You know how it is between us, Nazia. I can't speak with him right now."

"But you're still coming?"

She draws a breath and holds it, releasing it in bursts.

"Yes," I emphasize. "I'm too far away from Kingston to make the flight. It doesn't even make sense to go on."

"But you're still coming?"

In the background I can hear Kwabena's voice: "Is that for me?"

"What should I say?" she whispers.

"Tell him no."

I hold my breath as she obeys.

"How do you think he will take it?" I ask.

"I don't know. It is hard to say."

"Okay. Good-bye."

I have not prepared myself for the interview. When Frances left I kept a knapsack with some scripts and books.

I find a tree and sit on an uplifted root, marveling at the enduring beauty of *Geechee*, which was written at St. Regis. Like most of his plays, it has never been produced.

Kwabena had been teaching at St. Regis for a year when I arrived. His doctorate was in history; still, at the time of my arrival he was famous for his plays.

On my ride across America I contemplated my pretensions— so I was well placed on my arrival to notice his.

He always dressed in black and would ride around the campus on a purple Schwinn, hopping off and moving with a practiced slouch, a rounding of the torso that combined with endless legs to execute a question sign—a walking enigma.

Kwabena was born in Ghana and lived there until he was twelve years old. His father was the novelist Phineas Small, a contemporary of Wright and Ellison who had been born in Kumasi to missionaries from South Carolina.

In many ways my friendship with Kwabena was inevitable. We were young black men who worked in the theater. We were connected to Africa directly by blood. And we had spent our childhoods overseas in poor countries.

But in other ways we were not designed to get along. He was a born-again Christian, a Pentecostal, and I had come of age in Jamaica, where Christians and Rastafarians had fought a bitter cultural war. Jamaica is officially a Christian country, and open Rastafarians were persecuted, fired from their jobs, expelled from schools, trimmed by the police, banned from nightclubs, accused of being thieves and childnappers.

The Pentecostals and the Rastafarians were competing for the spirits of the poor. On top of this there were the conflicts in my family. No. I was not designed to be Kwabena's friend.

But I heard from students that he was a man of grace and a teacher of keen wisdom who took the time to help them shape their work, that he gave them confidence to reach inside themselves and launch their clipped imaginations in flight. So I gave him a chance. He told me that he was looking for a running partner and I accepted, and during our six-mile morning runs I discovered that his students were right.

One morning as we ran I asked him, "How does a guy like you become born-again?"

"What is a man like me?" he asked.

"You were born in Africa. You are a professor of history. You know that African people were Christianized by force. How do you reconcile that?"

"I have what I call the 'best bet' theory of Christianity," he said as we bounded down the stairs in the little football stadium. The field was bright and green below us. On the bright red running track a hurdler was practicing his form. "It's a simple thing. Everybody needs a moral compass. Now, a lot of religions will give you that, I will agree; but there is a funny little thing with Christianity. If you choose Christianity and Christianity is wrong then you're okay. Hinduism and Buddhism don't have a heaven or a hell so it doesn't really matter. And if the Jews or the Muslims are right then you can make a reasoned appeal to Allah or Yahweh that you share the prophets. But if Christianity is right and you're not a Christian, man, you're it."

When I met him, Kwabena might have known a lot about religion and the mechanics of faith, but he did not understand the stage.

He had devised something he called a theater of empathy, a theater based on Christian ideals that was supported by the members of the student Christian fellowship, whose members volunteered their time as actors and technicians in the service of the Lord.

Kwabena didn't understand the theater. He understood the force of metaphor, metaphor in language; but he did not understand the most important metaphor, the metaphor of the stage.

He did not understand the how and why of making bodies into poems, of giving bodies life beyond ideas, the how and why of making bodies move and stand in contrast with each other, the how and why of making conflicts out of shape and silence. And bodies, not language, form the essence of the stage.

Kwabena believed in me. When I spoke he would listen. He had never been to drama school or taken classes in directing or the theater arts. Everything he knew about the stage he had read and then observed. And I had studied with Gillespie.

On our morning runs, I would share with him the seeds that I had harvested from Peter Brook, Jerzy Grotowski, Stanislavsky, and Brecht, sometimes throwing them in his face to blind him as we fought religious wars. How could I not have known that he would pick them up and store them?

The truth is that Kwabena does not know the stage as well as I. But this is neither here nor there. The larger truth is that Kwabena is a poet, and no matter what I want to say, language is the essence of the stage.

With time, the bodies will fade from memory. They will grow weak and age, but the words will find a way of staying alive, staying fresh, renewing themselves and turning that dull dark spot of wood and flowing sheets into something impossibly graceful and lyrical.

Words . . . words . . . Kwabena has words. I concede this once again while reading *Geechee*.

There is a scene that has haunted me for days . . . the music of the lines, the poetry, and the startling image of Afua, a small black woman, standing on the open stage with the sound of the sea breaking around her, the horror of a lynching still sticky in her head, the threat of the shedding of her own blood in the naked machete that dangles in her hand as she remembers the dungeon in the castle where she slept before the horror of the crossing.

I can see her. I can smell her. I can see where he would place her ... downstage, her body heaving, her breasts moving, the tendons in her arms twitching, her eyes bloodshot, as these words stream out of her, eddying with the cadence of Gullah:

Above us is granite. Below us the give of wood seasoned with constant blood, piss, shit, vomit, sweat—our essence seeping out of us. We left our souls behind in that last light of the courtyard where two children stood crying without tears. We watched, as one, the way our souls lifted with the stench of our fear, trying to catch the current back to the ancient shrine. The children howled, wooden shackles tethering them, their nakedness a smudge on the pale white of limestone. We crawled, soulless but with the suggestion of song, into our tomb. Beyond this the burial repeated in ritual efficiency: the cave, the hull, the strange ocean. Sometimes in the blues I hear that dry, hollow cry; it is the wail from the granite cave caught in midflight. A woman wants to go back to hold those children, to hold them and comfort them, to hold their bodies to hers. Why must a woman stay in this hell, why must she not lift her wings and fly? Why?

(A voice calls from within)

VOICE: *Afua! Afua!*

AFUA: *Don't ask me to stay here—don't ask me. Kiss me, steel blade. Kiss me, Ogun's scepter. Kiss me, Oya, with the foam of your spit. Drag me back.*

How can I not envy this grace? How can I prevent this interview from degrading into hypocritical banter? How will I conceal my envy? What if something starts to pulse inside me and I feel the need to gloat, to reduce him to feel better about myself?

I want him to shine. But in his reflection I will see my face. I might be sad. I might be smug.

I can hear the engine of the Alfa in the distance. Frances has returned.

CHAPTER FOURTEEN

A killing tool in a woman's hands is surprisingly erotic. And no weapon is sexier than the knife, the close-quarter killer that can be summoned to hand and plunged into your heart and cranked and turned until you slump into a pool of your own wetness.

In the stabbing is the echo of the hot, hard screw . . . bodies grip and wrench and rail, searching for the switch that hitches time, that jacks it like a hiked-up skirt and brings it to a halt.

Frances knows how to wield a knife. We are sitting in the shade of a mango tree near the edge of the cliff, balancing on our knees a sheet of plywood covered with banana leaves.

From the wicker basket at her feet, she picks an avocado and weighs it in her palm. In her other hand she holds the carving knife that travels in her glove compartment.

With unnerving coolness Frances holds the avocado's neck and gores its fat, green belly, cleaving through its yellow flesh.

With her bangles jangling, she carves it, sculpting thick, striped wedges that resemble small canoes.

She reaches down again for plum tomatoes, severs their tips and dices them, adding from the basket lettuce, cucumbers, green peppers, an otaheite apple, carrots, a small papaya, and two carambolas, all of which she tosses with the avocado in a gourd.

Now she stops to rinse her hands with bottled water and begins to make a dressing. She peels a thumb of ginger, then pounds the glistening gristle with the handle of the knife and scrapes the juicy mash into a jar.

Into the jar she streams some Red Label, a local wine, what looks like olive oil, black pepper, and lime juice.

Then just as I'm sure that she's outdone herself and is capable of doing no more, the lovely and charming Frances Olivia St. Margaret Carey, who was born in Accra, Ghana, on February 11, 1963, and came to live in Jamaica with her father in 1981 at the age of seventeen after a cataclysmic argument with her mother hands me a paper bag containing a penknife with a fork attachment and a warm baguette that she wrangled from a baker at a hotel near Port Maria.

Keeping the carving knife, she invites me to eat, and as she picks a tomato wedge off the tip of the blade, my spirit becomes aroused and I feel a hidden part of me demanding blood sacrifice to bless this moment.

After lunch, we use the crumbling steps in the rock face to descend to the wisp of beach between the cliff and the water's edge. Like marzipan, the sand is damp and creamy. Yellow fish flutter in the shallows. Coconut trees with trunks like jet streams surge toward the sky, fronds awry like fireworks caught on film, and guarding a cave in the base of the cliff is a gnarled and ancient sea grape tree. There, in its shade, on a mound of compact sand, we sit, relax, and listen to our breathing, to the gulls, to the old tree rustling in counterpoint to the sea's accordion song.

"The Hora," she explains to me, "believe in the power of sound. The world is like a giant orchestra . . . and every *nonna* . . . everything, then . . . is like an instrument. And not just people—

animals and plants and stones . . . everything. And they all have a sound. And just as instruments in an orchestra need to get tuned to stay in harmony, people have to get tuned to stay in harmony with the world. There is this force inside all of us . . . *iz*. It's our reference point for tuning. Whenever you are feeling out of tune with the universe all you have to do is take the time to retune. And for that you need quiet. Being tuned means reaching a point where you are in sync with the universe, the grand orchestra. When you are in tune you can see spirits, talk to plants and rocks and have them talk to you and teach you. You can see the future. But it is a constant struggle. Very few people remain in tune for a long time, though. It's like being a piano in the tropics."

As I sit here now I'm feeling a heightened awareness. It's neither theory nor abstraction. I can hear clouds colliding. Ants skimming over grass. Coral growing. Sundrops crashing to earth. But then I have been smoking.

I ask her how she tuned me. The words emerge humbly, earnestly. Something—and I haven't determined what—has drawn me into a different space.

"Everything in the universe is connected," she explains. "And when people are truly in love they're connected in special ways. Yes, I'm telling you now again that I love you." She shuffles around in front of me, takes our hair, three feet of hers and two-and-a-half of mine, and begins to make a braid. "How did I tune you? You and I are playing a duet . . . and as we're grooving I heard that you were badly out of tune. And I stopped the music and gave you a reference note."

"So you love me then?"

She doesn't reply. She just continues braiding our hair, humming as she goes along, aware, I'm sure, of the ritual symbolism of this act of binding.

"So you love me then?" I ask again.

"Do you really need me to answer that?"

Rising to her feet, Frances dusts the sand off her clothes and stands in front of me, her form and features thrown in shadow by the brightness of the sky.

"Do I love you?"

Her voice is low and introspective, poised on the arc between release and restraint, ambiguous but not ambivalent. "Of course I love you, sweet boy. Completely. Without doubt, denial, or fear. And I know you love me, too. Come here . . . I want to feel my skin against yours."

Frances Carey understands the art of seduction, knows how to set a mood, knows how to conjure satin sheets and candle gloam with ordinary words like *come* and *here*. The words are not just spoken, they are delivered . . . timed, modulated, and phrased to invoke the power and mystery of the vulva, the door to the unseen from which we are formed, the threshold to the darkness to which we are eventually released.

Staring through the shroud of hair, she reveals herself slowly like the solution to an ancient riddle.

Her breasts are eggplants, watermelons, cacao pods. Sacks of yams. Tamarind balls. Anthills of the savanna.

I remove my shirt and embrace her, aroused by the heat of her nipples, the give of her breasts, the scoop of her sweat-damp belly.

"Do I love you?" she asks.

My fingers find a wetness . . . a fatness fills my palm . . . like a fruit . . . like something tree-ripened that strained then broke the twig. I can feel the gash where it fell against a stone. I dip into the mush to get a taste.

"Do you love me?"

We seek the sanctuary of the cave. The roof is low. The walls are tight.

"Do I love you?" she asks.

"Do you love me?"

She plants her palms on my belly, digs her heels into the sand.

"Do I love you?"

"Do you love me?"

She winces at the plunge, catches her breath.

"Do I love you?"

"Do you love me?"

The flesh gives way to the seed.

"Do I love you?"

"Do you love me?"

"Of course I love you. Of course I love you. You're the first man I ever loved. The first one I ever kissed. The last man that I would sleep with, fuck, screw, or make love to on my last night on earth. Every man I've been with has been a rehearsal for you."

"So you love me, then?"

"Yes, I love you."

"Why?"

"It's the only way I know how to feel about you. Breed me," she says. "Breed me. I want to have your child."

"Breed you when? Right now? Here? Now? This minute."

"No. Tonight. Breed me. Breed me. In my house. In my bed. On my sheets. Lover, come home and breed me."

CHAPTER FIFTEEN

We race toward her house, the engine whining like a clipper, the hood of the Alfa sharp and low, planing down the landscape, fading hills into fields and shadowy forests, shoveling the present, mowing the past, carving a path to the future.

From the field by the sea, we continue west, then turn off on the Junction Road, cresting to a tableland encrusted with bananas, up into the creviced hills.

Here the road is tighter and more rutted, with as many undulations as the river in the plunge beyond the low retaining wall.

We pass a lot of settlements along the way: wood-and-concrete bungalows in mud-washed white and shades of blue, clinging to the grade above a one-room shop with wooden stilts or concrete blocks to keep it level.

At Castleton, a district on the border of the parish of St. Andrew, some twenty miles from Kingston, the settlements give way to hamlets—a superette, a bar, a primary school, a church without a steeple—flanking the road in double file, slack but awe-inspiring, like guerrillas on parade.

Then a few miles on, past Golden Spring—a bar, a service station, a discotheque, a record shop—we come to Elder River.

From the Junction Road, the streets of Elder River trace a dartboard on the valley floor. In the middle there is a park; around the park a traffic circle; and around the traffic circle coils of residential streets. From the hills around the valley, narrow lanes come fluttering down, pooling by the park like streams of water.

Our clothing damp with rain, we make our way by one of them, in second gear to the sound of crunching gravel, the air smelling of earth, the earth smelling of sky, the sky smelling of sun like a sheet hung on a line.

Where the hill was cut to make the road the soil is reddish brown. Beyond the cut, the land resumes its graceful arc, swooping down then spreading out, a thing of simple beauty like a velvet cape unfurled.

In a dip by a tall hibiscus bush the road begins to wriggle and the town begins to flicker through a screen of trees.

There is no quaintness here—no shingled roofs or lattice trim or double doors with frosted panes. This is a town without illusions—a working town for working people trying to work their way through life, a town that doesn't pause to pose for pictures.

Up close the leafy park is shaded by a canopy of trees, and the grass is thin but shaggy. Curbing the park is a low stone fence—white with navy accents—and around this is a drainage ditch without a grate.

The buildings on the park are low, largely from the fifties: concrete, mainly cream and blue, with awnings, slab roofs, jalousies, burglar bars, and, quite surprising, a great amount of florid signs for simple kinds of business—bulk syrup, animal feed, propane cylinders, notions. For extra things, like mail or gas, the nearest place is Golden Spring. A movie means a journey into Kingston, fourteen miles away.

There was a time, I admit as we negotiate the town in silence, when this kind of town would bother me. Then I wanted the towns on this island to be as charming as the ones in the France of the lost generation—with oak trees and fountains and men discussing art and politics over streams of wine in bars whose walls of stone were soaked with memories of wars and epic heroes.

The resting place of heroes is not the grave, but the pages of books, and the chorus of songs, and the climactic scenes of plays.

And herein lies the tragedy of slavery.

The real tragedy of slavery is not material; the Africans who were cargoed in the holds of ships lost more than land and gold. They lost their myths and legends. And we, their sons and daughters, have emerged from this experience with cracked imaginations. And what is the imagination but the casing of the soul, the part of us unfettered by space and time, the part of us that dreams, that tells us what we were and what we are and what we can achieve?

But at this very moment, a man in Nigeria—let's call him Wole—is completely assured that his life is on the verge of change because yesterday at sunrise he poured a palm wine libation and asked an ancestor for help.

As he knelt, hands raised, palms turned to the sky, Wole fixed his inner gaze on the face of his great-grandfather's great-uncle—let's call him Femi—a stock fish trader and carver of wood who died of old age in the late nineteenth century.

Wole has never seen Femi, has never even seen a picture, yet he knows him as well as he knows his present next-door neighbor, because Femi, like all of Wole's ancestors, was inscribed and affirmed in Wole's memory through the songs and poems and legends of his family, his clan, his tribe.

But here, across the Atlantic, in this brutal foster care, we call on our ancestors as performance—a kind of acting out, a way to bluff the world that we have options. But we really don't believe, because in our darkest hours—in pain, in sickness, confusion, or despair—we forget the language of Kwanzaa and pray in the language we know to the power we feel. And that power is Jesus. And not just any Jesus. Not the colored one in the Afrocentric store, but the Jesus of our childhood, the blond-haired fairy prince.

In the absence of enduring myths we've tried to make our own, tried to reinvent a past that will assure us in this present. So one of us said that the white man was invented by a mad black scientist . . . another one said that Haile Selassie was God on earth . . . while another one informed us that we're the chosen ones, the Old Testament Jews sent to till the fields of Georgia—myths as simple and comforting as porridge . . . myths of a people still in trauma from the knowledge that their prophets could not part the sea and bring them home . . . myths of a people still astonished by the ease with which their brothers sold them into slavery, paraphrasing the narrative of Joseph.

And this is why Frances and I have been driving in silence: I discovered that she doesn't have the answers, that she is just as confused as I am. That she is, in fact, a liar.

● CHAPTER SIXTEEN

Arguments, like hurricanes, begin as small depressions.

As Frances stayed behind to gather shells to make a necklace, I went to the car to call Kwabena from my mobile phone.

I was confused.

I had an expectation—based on books and movies—that spiritual renewal was experienced through the eyes, that you shut your lids, reviewed your soul, and then resumed your outward gaze to find a world appearing different . . . brighter . . . dimmer . . . shrouded . . . scrubbed.

But when I staggered from the cave, the newness of the world was an experience of the skin . . . my feet against the sand, my beard against the breeze, the sun drops rolling down my pores. I felt as if my body had been rubbed with lime and pepper.

I had to talk about this newness with someone. And although I was avoiding him, Kwabena was the only choice. He knew me. He knew religion. He knew Africa.

What I did not know was that he knew Frances Carey, perhaps in the biblical way.

"Hello."

"Kwa—"

We lost the connection. I was sitting on a rock beneath the mango tree where Frances and I had eaten.

"So you're still coming today?" he asked.

From his voice I could not tell if he had spoken to Nazia.

"Well, I'm sort of delayed."

Chuckling, he said: "With whom?"

"Why 'whom' and not 'why'?"

"With you they are the same."

His voice was light and eager, which made me apprehensive. What if he dismissed my feelings?

Thunderheads were gathering. The light began to dim. The birds began to rustle. And I became distracted by how quickly showers form in the tropics. Without warning, clouds began to charge across the sky in columns, puffing darts of rain.

"So are you coming?" he asked again.

I glanced toward the water.

"Yeah. Of course. But I am going to be a little delayed. Like maybe tomorrow or the day after that."

"Well," he said in a passably optimistic tone, "just keep me posted. You're a grown man. Your business is your business. And you're handling your business, right?"

"Yes, sir. I am."

"Savor it and tell me all about it when you come."

"This is one you won't believe, Kwabena."

"I have heard that one before."

"You don't understand. I know where and with whom I want to spend the rest of my life."

"But doesn't she have a husband?"

"Who?"

"The producer."

I had forgotten Amaranta.

"Not her. Someone very different. A woman by the name of Frances Carey."

"I see."

"You see what?"

"Just . . . I see."

"What . . . do you know her?"

"Unfortunately, yes."

"You must be kidding."

"No, I'm not."

"You know her?"

"Do I know her? She was the last person I was with before Nazia."

My legs began to tremble. I tried to stand.

"Tell me that you're joking."

"But that was a long time ago," he said apologetically, as if my shock was his fault. "I'm sure that she is different now. I know that I have changed."

In my head I thought I heard him reminiscing. And the fact that he knew her better than I began to tinge my voice with envy.

"But that was a long time ago," he said easily. A little easier and I would have believed that he was trying to spare my feelings. Harsher and I would have believed that he was trying to compete. "I have known her almost all her life," he continued. "Her father was a law lecturer at the University of Legon. My father was lecturing in English. We practically grew up as brother and sister. And when we moved back to the States she used to come and visit us. It was a little foolishness, Carey. A little foolishness that lasted for a year."

A year is a significant amount of time, I thought, yet Kwabena had never mentioned Frances, and he had shared with me the details of his life before he was married. When I met him at St. Regis he was celibate and single. Why had he not mentioned her? And why was he watching her videotape when I stumbled through his door?

"Why did you break up?" I asked.

He chuckled at my tone, which was huffy.

"Maybe you should ask her," he replied. "I would be interested in what she had to say."

"This is not her business," I told him.

"Well, the truth is that it's not my business either."

I stood up and began to walk around the tree in circles.

"I'm sorry," I muttered. "I didn't mean to sound that way."

My apology unplugged something inside him.

"We broke up over sex," he confessed.

"Oh," I said, a little short of breath, "you were going too fast?"

"No," he emphasized. "It was the other way around. She wanted sex and I couldn't go there because I was a Christian."

For a while I could not speak. Could not think. Could see only smoky pictures of naked flesh . . . and silver sweat . . . and hear a guitar with a wah-wah warble fading out and in.

"How old were you?" I managed.

"I was seventeen and she was fourteen."

"Oh."

In my head I began to do the math. This amount of men for that amount of years . . . more than my toes and fingers.

"But, Carey, you have to understand how we got together to understand how we broke up."

"Okay then, tell me."

"Frances and I didn't have a typical relationship, if there is such a thing. There was a real sense of convenience about it. You see, I was very insecure when my family moved back to America. I felt like a stranger here. And as I am adjusting to this new idea of home, working through the turmoil of where I fit in, Frances is sent to spend a year with us because she's giving her parents grief. So there it is, two people in a strange country, two people who have a history. That is how it happened. We both had a sense of difference. We were both into books. And for a while it was everything I wanted. Then she told me that she wanted me to help her lose her hymen. And we found ourselves with a problem."

I was drawn into the beauty of the reminiscence, and for a moment I forgot that the woman with whom my best friend used to be in love was the woman I loved today, and to comfort him I offered: "She wanted to show you how much she loved you—that's all—by giving you a beautiful thing."

"No, it was nothing like that," he dismissed. "She was biding her time with me. She was using me. She was really into this older guy who kept turning her down because he wanted a woman with experience. She was trying to use me, Carey. She just wanted me to pave the way, offering me the role of John the Baptist when I wanted to be Jesus."

"So there she was with her plans laid out," I said with a nervous laugh, relieved that things had gone no further, "and God came along and spoiled them."

We laughed, but his voice was constricted.

"Are you guys okay now? Do you talk?"

"When we broke up that was it. I have never seen her in all these years."

"But she was such a—"

"Because it was not important," he insisted. "It was a little teenage thing."

But that time, at your house, I wanted to ask, why were you watching her on TV? Does Nazia know who she is?

"So you two met?" he said flatly.

"Yes."

"And one thing led to another." He began to sound a little smug. "One blind person led the other in a dark room, and they mistakenly took off each other's clothes."

"She's a wonderful woman," I defended, as I scratched a spot between my shoulder blades. "Times change. People move on."

Kwabena withdrew into silence.

"What?" I asked, weakly.

"Nothing . . ."

"It can't be nothing. What?"

I was not prepared for his reply.

"Carey, you don't know her," he shouted. "She will lead you on and wreck your life. Frances Carey is a fucking flake. She has never committed to anything in her life. Have you lost your fucking mind?"

I had never heard him curse before.

"Listen to me," I argued. "How did this come to be about you? I called you to share something wonderful that just happened to me. I have never felt this way before, Kwabena. Forget all the bullshit that has gone on in the past. This woman has led me to a place where I have come to understand myself, and that is all that counts."

"Understand yourself how?" he challenges.

"I am thinking of converting."

"To what?"

"Her religion."

"So the rastaman is going to be a Catholic."

"She isn't Catholic," I say timidly to a man who knows my woman in a fundamental way. "She is Hora."

"Oh, that is completely bogus, Carey. Frances doesn't take it seriously. Lemme just explain something to you before you go and fuck your life. If there is one thing I know about Frances it is this. She will do and say anything to get a man to fuck her. That is how she was. That is how she is. That is how she will always be."

And as Kwabena thundered in my ear, the subject of his fusillade came running through the grass, arms flailing with excitement in the wind and what was now a driving rain, shoulders swinging side to side, hair unfurled, laughing as she called my name, pointing to the car.

The roof was down. Water groggled on the seats.

I closed my eyes and felt her hug me, her tongue inside my gaping mouth.

"Lightning's going to strike us, Carey. Hang up. Quick, we have to go. I'll race you to the car."

"Frances, you know Kwabena Small?"

"Yes," she said defensively. "Why do you want to know?"

"I have him on the phone."

She sucked her teeth and muttered, and I felt her warmth begin to pull away.

"Frances . . . Frances . . . Frances." The water had soaked my clothes. "Frances . . . Frances . . . Frances."

"What is he saying?" she challenged. "What is he fucking saying?"

She grabbed the phone and smashed it on the mango tree. I could not find the muscles that would open my eyes.

"How dare you, Carey? How dare you!"

"Frances . . . Frances . . . Frances. What does all this mean?"

"How dare you, Carey? How dare you!"

"Frances . . . Frances . . . Frances."

"Carey!"

"Frances!"

Then I staggered. Frances Carey had hit me.

CHAPTER SEVENTEEN

Over the Atlantic, shoes off, seat back, legs up, I focus on my breathing, trying to keep a wave of guilt from washing up along my spine, bringing with it memories of the way that my ancestors came across this sea . . . in ships . . . in fear . . . in chains . . . as loot . . . unloved . . . debased and then renamed.

Of what real consequence are my troubles? If I should scream right now someone would comfort me. If I die they would not cast me out. If I need to pee, I can.

But still, my skin begins to bead with sweat. Still each breath is tight—constricted and explosive like a sneeze.

"Mr. McCullough, are you okay?"

The flight attendant takes my hand. The pupils of her hazel eyes are gaping. With furrowed brows I try to tell her that she would not understand. But she continues to touch me, crow's-feet gripping the edges of her eyes.

Over my shoulder, beyond the cabin divider, a child begins to cry, and a voice begins to hum "Amazing Grace" . . . a grandmother's voice . . . a voice as comforting and simple as hush puppies, and as the crying falls away the flight attendant pats my shoulder.

From across the aisle, a sympathetic voice addresses me.
"First time?"

Two women nod politely. The closer one has sunburned skin
that loops around her neck in pleats. Her friend, whose oblong
jaw is sturdy as a brick, is staring from above a Jackie Collins
novel.

They are simple women. I know them without knowing.
They buy their clothes at Wal-Mart and have Sunday brunch at
Shoney's, and have between the two of them a year of junior
college. Yet they feel the right to ask me if I've ever flown before, these two women who were placed in business class because the flight was oversold.

No, I will not answer them. And I will show them no anger.
They are simple women. They would not understand.

Through the thinning clouds I get a glimpse of South Carolina, draped in the familiar plaid of the South—green fields
crossed by red dirt roads and blacktop highways striped with
white, a place where the right-angled patterns of history are
resistant to change.

From the air, Columbia is a dull gray stain, a stain lacking the
confidence of presence. But how could it, positioned as it is in
relation to water that carries the history of a nation in its mud?
In South Carolina, America's past is a constant present. Close
your eyes and breathe deeply and the lingering aroma of the
Civil War dead comes drifting off the misty swamps.

A walk into the swamps between Sumter and Columbia is a
journey into history . . . into the world of Confederate pride, of
slaves eking out a living in a world they did not make—a world
of simple suffering.

One morning, years before my fateful journey, I went for a
walk along the swamps and found myself along a path I did not
know. There I saw a woman on the bank of a river, her head
bandannaed, her body bent and broken with age, catching fish
in the mist as she would have done in another time.

Sensing my presence, she turned and nodded, and I smiled and whispered something in patois, realizing after the words had gone that I was not in Jamaica, but somewhere deep in America's heart where time no longer mattered.

At first the woman was startled, then she smiled, and nodded her head ... seemed to understand. And although I saw her only briefly, and from a distance, and through mist, I can still see her face today, the lines of sorrow carved in her cheeks, the tiredness and patience of her eyes. All these things remain with me like dreams.

The airport is small tiny, even after recent renovation: long walls in light grays, rows of plastic seats, fast-food restaurants, and clothing stores that won't attract you if you haven't lost your luggage.

I am the last to leave the plane. Ahead of me, beyond the empty counters, people greet each other tiredly, casually, then make small talk as they gumper to the moving walkway at the end of the hall, which is carpeted in blue. There, a little girl is sprinting to her mother, who lumbers ahead then stops with just enough oxygen to open her arms and smile. She catches the girl, lifts her high, ignoring her husband, who is slim and fit, but did not choose to run. With my knapsack on my shoulder I follow this American tragedy, unprepared but ready to meet my situation.

He is sitting in a dark blue chair, dressed in khakis and a yellow polo shirt.

If this were day the sun would have been shining through the skylight panels to illuminate his greatness. But under these fluorescent bulbs he is not one of America's greatest living playwrights—just a thin, round-shouldered man with the shaven head and goatee of an athlete, peering over reading glasses at a book.

My contact lenses are sticking to my eyes. No, these could not be tears.

From a firm handshake Kwabena draws me to his chest, which smells of citrus-based cologne.

He taps my bag.

"Is this it?"

"I'm traveling light."

Outside, the purpling sky is smeared with red and gold. The air feels like a blanket. The lot recalls a tally sheet: short strokes with long lines running through. I have a heavy debt to pay.

"When you called me from Jamaica," he says, opening the door of his white Buick Regal, "you said you'd be delayed. I was thinking by a day or two. Not that this is not a good time or anything. I just have to juggle some things around."

I toss my knapsack in the back between a pair of booster seats. The red velour is damp. The rug is brown with dirt and juice. Cardboard books and sippy cups are tucked behind the driver's seat.

"That was two weeks ago, wasn't it?"

"Time flies when you're having fun."

He leans against the car, gazing into space . . . at the sky . . . at the red stars shifting like ants. Like me, he is sweating from the heat. In the humid air my shirt collapses on my skin.

"Time flies," he says, without looking at me.

"Yeah," I reply. "I'll explain the whole thing later."

He brings his watch to his nose. Squints at the time.

"Darkness comes so fast sometimes," he mutters to himself.

I don't know what to say to this. Is this his way of asking me to drive?

"Where are the keys?" I ask.

He gets behind the wheel. He does not answer.

I've been rehearsing this drive for days. Yet as we lurch onto the highway I still can't find the language or the frame of mind with which to tell him of the things that I have seen and done.

Although I met him late in life, no one knows me better. My brother, father, mirror, priest, he knows my dirty history: knows how many women I've been through, knows how many women I've hurt, knows how many women I've seduced then gotten bored with, knows how many women I've lied to, knows how many women I've lied to myself about loving; and most importantly, he knows Frances. And when I tell him the story of the past two weeks I know what he will do: He will listen and smile and nod and inquire—but he will not take me seriously. Not this time. For the whole thing will sound like an elaborate lie, a fanciful tale from a desperate man who once again, following a pattern as sure as an engraving, allowed a woman to confound his life.

And what about the interview for the *Sunday Times*? He will ask this. And I will have to tell him that the editor lost her patience and dropped me from the series. So the story of Kwabena Small will not be written. At least not for now.

Carey McCullough, you are a waste of sperm. You—more than anyone in the world—should understand Kwabena's situation. Because you know what happens when the human mind begins to break under a burden . . . the body begins to resent itself . . . it doesn't care how it looks, it doesn't care how it's dressed, if it is washed, what it eats, how much of what it drinks, where it sleeps, in what position, next to whom. And after a while, the soul, concerned about its own preservation, begins to think of ways to launch itself into flight.

Right here, along this very road, seven years ago, your soul arced across this very sky, fluttering behind your scream like a flustered woman begging her husband to return.

This must never happen to Kwabena. He has a wife and four children and, unlike me, a good heart.

As we pull into a service mart I notice that the car is dim.

I begin to glance around me—at the floodlights spurting on the gas pumps, the reflections off the side of a low-rider truck.

And as I become aware of the smells of the place: petrol, muffler fumes, spilt beer, and, as a family returns to their car with a paper plate, chicken warmed up in a convection oven, it comes to me—the dash lights are out.

"Fly the hood so I can take a look at the fuse box," I offer.

"I'll get around to it," he replies, watching the family go by, taken, it seems, by the mother's rolling bottom. "Do you want anything?"

He is still holding the steering wheel. He is speaking to me without looking.

"What are you getting?"

I make a point of turning toward him. He glances.

"I'm gonna try my luck with the lottery."

"Okay, then. Some juice."

As he leaves the car I switch on the radio in the middle of a preacher's rant: "Men, you have got to take charge. It is your godly responsibility. You have got to say, 'Let's pray.' You have got to say, 'None of that in my house.' You have got to. Too many men rely on their wives to do that. Too many men. Take charge. Tell her what to do. God has put you in charge—"

I shake out my locks and turn it off. I open the window for air.

"Do you have a tape or anything?" I call after him.

"The radio eats them up."

He shrugs and walks away.

A moment later, through the plate-glass window of the super mart, I see Kwabena whip his palm with a wad of lottery tickets, urging on his luck.

He lost his house six months ago. Now he lives in a house that was owned by his grandfather, a physician from the low country, who established a medical mission in Ghana in the 1920s.

Kwabena never told me that he lost the house. He simply told me that he would be moving. I know the story from Nazia. He knows that I know the truth, but we have never discussed it. What would be the point?

Kwabena lost his house because he loves the theater. In addition to teaching at Willingmore he had built a community theater group in Ridgeland, an area of desperate poverty in Jasper County, the poorest county in the state. Over the years he had taught petty marijuana dealers how to run a lighting grid, motivated teenage mothers to get up off the couch on the listing porch and learn to build a set, inspired parents who had lost their pride when the mills closed down to support their children's talent. He had touched a community of disenfranchised people with the power of his art.

But he could not afford it. Ridgeland is three hours from Columbia. Kwabena used to go there every Saturday morning. The group rented space in the back of a pool hall. To cover their expenses, Kwabena tried to raise money in different ways. He wrote grant proposals. He organized raffles and talent shows. In the meantime he financed the group out of his pocket.

When the owner of the pool hall told the group that he was going to sell the building, Kwabena refinanced his home and bought it. According to Nazia he had planned to hold it till he found another buyer. He hoped. He prayed. He gambled. He lost.

Down on the highway, flashing lights remind me of the many complications of the South.

I have been harassed so many times: pulled over for offenses like driving too slowly, asked for permission to search my car, watched as dogs left their scent on my belongings, been taken aside and asked to make it easier by telling the truth.

You don't always feel angry when things like this happen. Most of the time you just feel embarrassed because you realize there was a moment in all of it when you fell into an ancient role, that you denied yourself the right to indignation, that you kept glancing in your mirror when your journey continued, that you held it in for as long as you could . . . then cried.

We resume the journey in a mood of contemplation, picking at the remnants of thoughts and dreams, trying to find shelter for our beleaguered souls.

We pass a sign that marks the exit to the house in which Kwabena used to live, the house to which I ran for refuge. I sense him waiting for a question, a recollection, something to acknowledge our past.

But I don't know what to say.

We leave the highway and begin to move along a secondary road. There are fields on either side of us, tall plants marching off in rigid columns into darkness.

It is a darkness I have rarely seen, a darkness like drifting snow. Until the headlights plow a path, the road appears to be obstructed.

The radio is off. Just below the engine's moan there is the sound of whirring tires and the creak and bounce of aging shocks.

"We should speak before we reach the house," Kwabena offers. He says this with the caution of a person who has chosen one of many unfamiliar roads.

He turns toward me, expecting an answer, but shame is crystallizing in my joints. I cannot move my head to look.

"Kwabena—"

"Carey—"

We drive along in silence.

"Small—"

"McCullough—"

Neither of us can spark a conversation. We are as useless as damp matches. And as I turn to try again, the car is filled with light and noise.

It is happening in slow motion. . . . Kwabena is heaving the wheel . . . we are skimming sideways like a snowmobile . . . through the window I can see the pulsing stars . . . then pain begins to glimmer in my skull in constellations.

"What the fuck was that?"

Kwabena flies his door and sprints toward the quickly fading lights.

He reappears with his hands on his hips, fatigued and frightened. He passes me without touching, his breathing tight. From somewhere close behind me I hear him suck his teeth and turn around. He pats my shoulder, leans against the car, slaps his thigh and holds his head, confounded.

"You know, I didn't see him," he mutters. "My mind was off somewhere. Did you see him?"

Perhaps I am in some kind of shock. Perhaps I am relieved by the distraction. Perhaps my brush with death has given me a sense of scale. But I am strangely calm.

"Did I see him?" I reply. "No, I didn't. Not until we went into the slide."

The car is perpendicular to the road, five feet of space on either side. How did the other vehicle pass? I cannot see the skid marks in the darkness. The effort strains my eyes. I look up at the sky to ease the strain of focus. Another mystery of life.

I lean against the driver's door. Kwabena moves away and sits down on the trunk, his heels up on the bumper.

"Carey, do you realize that we could have died? We could have left this place with hardened hearts. We could have gone without saying sorry. That's why we should never let things come between us, man. Time in this life is not guaranteed. That was a sign, my brother. A very big sign. We are not living right with each other, man. We are not living right at all. We have allowed things to come between us. And when you think about them, these are unimportant things. In the bigger scheme of life what is the *Sunday Times*? Who is Frances Carey? Why should I care what she is to you? Why should you care what she was to me? I am sorry, my brother. I am sorry, Carey. Don't harden your heart any more. Forgive me."

The car begins to shake. I move to hold him, to calm him down, to reassure him that I have forgiven him, that I am the one who needs to beg forgiveness, then I discover that I am the one who is crying.

The shudders are mine. I have been quiet because, like the man trying to quell a sneeze before it crests, my serenity was in fact suppression. I have been trying to avoid discussing something that I want to keep inside myself.

This is it: If I had died and my spirit had been faced with three tunnels of light—one for Rastafarians, one for Jews, and one for Christians—I would have put my trust in Christ.

The Jews await their Messiah. Selassie came and went. But Jesus saves.

The possibilities of each messiah are conjugated in a different tense. In Judaism it is future. In Rastafarianism it is past. In Christianity it is present. Jesus *saves*. Not then. Not soon. But now.

"Kwabena," I ask, "will you pray with me? I don't remember how to pray." He puts his arm around me. "I know that God will listen . . . but I don't know. . . ."

"It's okay," he whispers. "It's late and we have to get home."

"Do you know Psalm Fifty-one?"

"No."

"Just repeat after me."

Have mercy upon me, O God, according to Thy loving-kindness: according unto the multitude of Thy tender mercies blot out my transgressions.

Wash me thoroughly from mine iniquity, and cleanse me from my sin.

For I acknowledge my transgressions: and my sin is *ever before me.*

Against Thee, Thee only, have I sinned, and done this *evil in Thy sight: that Thou mightest be justified when Thou speakest,* and *be clear when Thou judgest.*

Behold, I was shapen in iniquity; and in sin did my mother conceive me.

Behold, Thou desirest truth in the inward parts: and in the hidden part *Thou shalt make me to know wisdom.*

Purge me with hyssop, and I shall be clean: wash me, and I shall be whiter than snow. . . .

● CHAPTER EIGHTEEN

The shower braces me.

Dressed, I tug the lacy curtains and familiarize myself with my surroundings, seeing clearly now the things that passed the night before as shifting blurs and shadows. In the distance is the sound of trains.

I have never been to this house before, but I know it without knowing, for British architects, like British soldiers, have traveled far and wide and left behind them scattered bands of handsome bastard children.

So this cottage—single room, brick construction, plaster walls, wooden floor, a chimney at one end—has siblings from Jamaica to South Africa and Pakistan.

It is simply decorated, with furniture I know: a beige love seat and sofa bed, a dresser and an armoire in unfinished pine, a glass-topped dining table, vinyl chairs with metal frames.

Forty yards away, separated from the cottage by a grove of trees and grass, is the butter-colored farmhouse where Kwabena lives.

According to Kwabena, it was built in 1891 on what was then

a wooded hill that overlooked the railway cut that marked the color line. The builder was a Boston anthropologist who had come to do research among the residents of what was then a separate negro town across the railway tracks.

When Kwabena's grandfather bought the house in 1922 it was abandoned in the middle of a forest in a racial no-man's-land. But when he returned to Columbia in 1946 after twenty years in Ghana, Shandon, one of the city's most exclusive neighborhoods, had grown within a mile of it; and the negro town over the hill, across the tracks had been absorbed into the city.

Last night as we ascended on a winding avenue of old shade trees I glimpsed details of a city reconstructed from the brimstones of the Civil War: Victorian porches, Gothic gables, Greco-Roman columns, all of them revivals.

We did not go to bed immediately. Instead we stayed up, talking late into the night about the production of the *The Tempest* he was mounting at the county jail in Greeleyville.

For the sake of relevance, Kwabena set the play in the low country, on a fictional sea island very much like St. Helena.

But in an early read-through, a brother by the name of Blow Dog remarked that the Duke of Milan reminded him of Moschino. Miss Raymond, the drag queen, commented that Prospero was just like Prada. Another inmate said that Caliban was nothing but a crack ho.

To maintain their enthusiasm, Kwabena encouraged the cast to help him shape the play.

Now the play is about a gang, dressed in Moschino, who turn up at the wrong club on the wrong night and run into the dancer with the onliest moves, who is dressed in Prada. The dancer has no backup but a crack ho by the name of Animal, who is played by an inmate who looks like Robert Downey, Jr.

The genius of the play, Kwabena said, is that in many ways it works. If only his students at Willingmore were as hungry or inventive. Willingmore was St. Regis all over again—a small school with rich kids who expected to be treated like guests at a good hotel.

Nazia is in the kitchen when I enter from the porch. It is Saturday. Kwabena has already left for Greeleyville.

The house is quiet. Outside there is a breeze. An overhanging tree begins to slur against the shingled roof. The air smells of cloves and curry with a top note of the lemon oil they use to subtilize the heirlooms . . . cabinets with crowns, spindled chairs, tables with folding leaves in walnut, oak, and cherry.

The children are asleep above me.

Seated at the kitchen table, Nazia is reading, a pile of books before her, silver glasses gnatted on her nose, a pencil in her mouth, a fist beneath her chin, her slender shoulders drawn up to her ears.

She has not seen or heard me.

Nazia was born in Uganda to a Pakistani family. Like me she had to flee her country in the dead of night. In 1972, when she was three months old, Idi Amin expelled Uganda's forty thousand Asians, most of whom had known no other country.

As I watch her from the doorway—the smoothness of her skin, the darkness of her eyes, her nose a slender finger pointing to her mouth—I am reminded of her youth.

Nazia is thirty. When she met Kwabena she was seventeen, waiting tables at her parents' restaurant in Queens. By then I had returned to NYU. Kwabena had come to New York to give a lecture at St. John's.

"I have found her," he said when I answered the phone.

"Who?" I asked.

"My wife."

I thought it was a joke. He was serious. They were married in a year. She was a virgin. He had been celibate for eighteen years. The children came before she had a chance to breathe. She has always been a full-time mother. Now she is taking summer courses at a local junior college.

She removes her glasses when she sees me. I sit across from her. She pats my shoulder.

"Sorry for going to bed before you came," she says. "But you know . . . the children. Plus, you and Kwabena have a lot to talk about, I'm sure. I heard you laughing like a pair of schoolboys. That is good. That is good. That is very, very good. Sometimes we human beings can handle things so badly, if you know what I mean. How are you, my friend?"

"I am fine."

Now that I have seen her this is true.

"You look well," she tells me, holding my chin and turning my face. She examines me from different angles, focused but indifferent, like a vet.

"He has forgiven you," she whispers, tilting her head as if the room is wired. So completely does Kwabena fill her life. "At first he was incredulous. He went to the airport and waited five hours. He just kept shaking his head when I asked him what happened. I knew it was bad. But not as bad as it became."

"What happened?"

She smiles and shakes her head to reassure me. It is the kind of courtly modesty displayed by concierges at the best hotels.

"I'm sorry."

"Oh, Carey, stop it." She waves away my fussiness. "It's not as if he's hard to deal with."

I lean toward her.

"Well," she continues conspiratorially, "he got a little angry. In fact I have never seen him this angry before. I asked him what happened maybe one time too much and he snapped at me." She inhales and holds her breath and looks away. When she looks again her face is set. "He trampled up the stairs and slammed the doors. The kids were frightened. They had never seen their father act like that before."

With a fingertip she wipes the inner corners of her eyes, then sets her elbows on the table, using her palms to brace her drooping face.

"Carey. What happened? Why did you take so long to call? You should have told him something. Anything. But you should not have left him in limbo like that."

"What did he tell you?"

I have to know this before I can answer.

"He has not told me anything."

This is delivered as a plea.

"I don't know what to tell you, Nazia."

"Okay then, Carey. Where have you been? You could have called me if you were afraid of facing him. I would have helped to smooth things over."

"I know. I know."

"So if you know why did you handle things this way? So messily? All of this could have been avoided. Do you know what it has been like in this house for the last two weeks?"

"Of course I don't."

"So my husband is incredulous. Then my husband is angry. Then you know what, Carey? My husband begins to doubt himself."

"Like what? Like how? Like what do you mean?"

"Like he starts to say things like, 'Oh, I shouldn't be in a situation where an interview like this should mean so much.' "

"Oh, fuck."

"This is very hard for him, Carey."

"It must be hard for you, too."

"Not really. I love my husband. The truth is that we have a roof over our heads. We never go to bed hungry and the children have more space to run around. I know what it is to really be displaced. This is not hard for me at all. What is hard is when I don't know how to comfort him. When I don't know what to say."

"He's angry with me."

"No. He's not. This morning when he came upstairs he woke me up and held my face and whispered as he giggled, 'Nazia, I'm so happy that he came.' "

With her thumb she whisks some water from my lashes.

"You have to understand that you have always been my husband's hero, the one who made the grade. Tell me, Carey, where were you?"

Later, in the cottage, I am distracted from my writing by a sound.

"Hello."

There is no answer. I go back to writing. Soon I hear the sound again: a shuffling, then a sort of grunt.

I open the door and look around, but there is nothing. But as I turn around I see a flash and feel a force and hear the iron doorknob cracking on the wall.

"Fucking Jesus Christ!"

Kwabena's body shudders in the grizzly suit.

"I couldn't resist," he says, removing the head. "When I got back from Greeleyville the kids were asking where was Uncle Carey and Nazia said he was probably writing and shouldn't be disturbed. Tano said, 'Oh, Daddy, maybe we should go and scare him.' It sounded like a great idea to me so I went over to Willingmore to get the suit."

"You are absolutely bizarre," I tell him through a laugh. "Where are the kids?"

"Nazia just took them down to soccer. You must be ready for lunch?"

On the back porch, over griddle cakes and lemonade, he tells me about the day's rehearsal.

"Oh, they added a great dance number. Blood Nice, who plays Trinculo, said that he was feeling Miranda like Jennifer Lopez. Another cat said that J Lo used to be a fly girl on *In Living Color* so, yeah, the dance routine could work. Well, Miss Raymond was ecstatic. When he gets out and does his lower surgery he plans to change his face to look like her."

"And did he scream out 'I was born to play this role'?"

"Of course he did."

The laughter drains away.

"I like this place," I say to keep us going.

"Me, too," he replies. "I just never thought I would ever have to live here."

"Don't worry about it, man."

"I'm not worried," he answers quickly.

I open my hands. "Well, there is nothing really to worry about."

"But I *am* worried about Nazia," he confides.

"Why is that?"

"She has taken it too easily."

"She's an easy person, and she loves you."

He looks toward the cottage, fixes his mind on a thought, then turns again to face me.

"The truth is that I feel as if I'm failing. Losing a house over your family's head is the kind of thing that stays with you. Nazia followed me home, and it has not worked out for her."

"Move to another state."

"What would be the point?"

He grinds his glass into the slatted redwood table, his forehead deeply ruffled.

"I am a prisoner of Eden, Carey. Look at all this."

"Don't say that, man."

"You have never lived here, Carey. For a while I thought my father was a coward when he left and went to Ghana. But now I understand him. Here, you're reminded of the power of white folks every day."

"So why did you come back?"

He drains his glass.

"Because it is my home."

He begins to cluck his tongue against his palate. He has opened up to me. Now he is staring, demanding that I do the same. He wants to know where I have been and he wants to know about what's going on with Frances.

But I am not ready to speak.

"I wish I had a similar sense of home," I tell him.

"Home is the place where you have to go for funerals. It ain't nothing more than that. Don't make it any bigger."

He winks and smiles.

"Kwabena—"

I am trying to find a way to talk to him about my spiritual journey without involving Frances.

"Go ahead," he says expectantly.

"What if I told you that my home might be in Africa?"

He sucks his teeth.

"I would say that sex is a powerful thing."

"I think that we should take this up another time."

I stay inside the cottage for the rest of the day. On Sunday evening Kwabena comes to ask if I am interested in dinner. I tell him no. Later on there is a softer knock.

"It's Nazia. Will you please come out and have something to eat?"

"I am not hungry."

"I have brought you dinner anyway."

"Where is your husband?"

"He had to go back to church."

"When is he coming back?"

"You are being very childish."

"Thank you for the compliment."

"I mean the both of you."

She walks around and looks in through a window. I am lying on the couch in boxers only.

"I used to look up to the both of you," she scolds, "and you are both so disappointing."

I sit up and lean forward with my elbows on my knees.

"Frig it. Bring the food."

"I am not your servant. I will leave it on the steps."

I twitch a shirt around my shoulders and hitch up my jeans, but she is gone when I reach the door. I do not call after her. She has left behind the scent of her perfume and a puzzling odor, like mentholated cigarettes.

I smell my shirt. It must be me. I have begun to smoke again.

CHAPTER NINETEEN

It is Friday, and I have not been out of the cottage. I am no longer angry. I am simply embarrassed. Nazia has been coming with meals and notes, and I have been ungracious.

The notes are from the children. They know that I am here. They know that there is something wrong. They sense that I have hurt their father.

"The both of you are ruining my life," says Nazia through the door.

After seeing me half-naked she does not come to the window.

"I am sorry," I reply. "Maybe I should leave."

"No. Don't do that. Then I would have no one to talk to."

"What do you mean?"

"He isn't speaking to me either. He thinks I am taking your side."

"But you're not."

"Of course I'm not. There is no side to take."

"Where is he now?"

"In the house."

"Where are the kids?"

"In the den."

"Take them out for a drive. Tell Kwabena that I'm ready to talk."

"For this to work," Kwabena tells me as we sit out on the porch, "the both of us will have to tell the truth."

Nazia has taken the children to the movies.

"And I think we also must agree that you will listen with an open mind."

"I will give you that."

He pours some iced tea in a frosted glass and takes his time to drink it, closing his eyes, drifting off into another world. When the tea is finished he cracks a cube of ice and spits the fragments in the glass, echoing the sound of broken teeth.

"So you feel as if your heart's in Africa?" he begins, continuing the conversation at the point at which I walked away.

"I wasn't just idling for those last two weeks," I emphasize. "I've been pondering some things that are important to me, to who I am and have been and might want to be."

He gestures with an open hand. He is wearing a gray T-shirt and khaki shorts. "I'm listening, Carey."

"What is it with us, Kwabena?"

"What is it with who?"

"Not just us, like me and you. But what is it with us? We know everything about slavery and the ways in which our gods were taken away from us. Yet we still cling to this thing called Christianity? What does that say about us, as writers, as artists, as thinkers, as leaders, as individuals, as a people?"

He shrugs. "It says that we are religious. What?"

"But you have always talked about your relationship to God as a kind of business deal. I don't get it. What I felt that night as we prayed by the car was not business, man. That was power."

He pours himself some more iced tea. My glass is empty.

"If I gave you the impression there was no kind of emotional force, then I am sorry. On the night I gave my life to Christ I felt a power working through me. And I still feel that power today. But the truth is that I didn't take the altar call. I sat there in my seat and made a deal. It wasn't a joke. It was serious business."

I begin to chuckle. He begins to laugh, and it becomes clear to the both of us that we have wandered to the place where our friendship was conceived—the crack between opposing points of view.

"You know that the idea of a transaction doesn't sound very spiritual," I say, taking the glass out of his hand. I drink from it and return it, and he pretends to disinfect it with his breath.

"Well, you know all about my best bet theory."

A wind begins to pick up. A sparrow darts beneath the eaves.

"So you came to it by accident. You chose it out of fear. But what is it that keeps you there? What is it that holds you?"

"I would have to say the teachings of Christ and the teachings of love."

"All that is well and good, Kwabena, but how do you as an African deal with slavery? How do you as an American deal with segregation?"

He claps his hands together and leaves them for a second, then releases them in a way that demands the appearance of a dove. He pours himself some more iced tea and offers me a glass by touching the jug.

"To do that you have to reach the place where you accept that flesh is fallible," he says. "If you judge any belief on the acts of the believer, you'll always be disappointed."

"That's not good enough for me, Kwabena. I am sorry."

The tendons in my neck, I know, are showing through my skin.

"But let's think about this, Carey. Christianity has a touchstone for perfection—and that is Christ. If Christ were racist and condoned all the beatings and the rapes and the tortures and the thievery, then Christianity would be useless. But he didn't.

He condemned these things. So those believers who did these things are failures—not Christ and not Christianity." He stops, drawn into himself by a memory it seems. "But having said all this," he continues, "these things have always been a challenge. I am compelled by the truth of the gospels but angered by the people who brought that truth to me."

"And how do you reconcile that?"

"I always remind myself to turn to the essential faith, the teachings of Christ, and let them be my guide. If I should reject Christianity, Carey, it wouldn't be because I was rejecting Christ. It would be a rejection of people like Thomas Jefferson and Columbus and Jesse Helms and Strom Thurmond who've done evil in His name."

"But if it is so good, Kwabena, and if God is so good, then how come he couldn't make good out of evil?"

He leans away from me on the cane-backed chair that belongs around the table in the kitchen. Holding my stare, he takes a long drink from the glass, which is sweating in the heat.

"Carey, the only answer I have is that I found that Christianity transformed me. So it comes back again to a personal thing."

"But look at this country, man. Look at this state. Look—"

"I know where you are going with it, Carey. The fact of the matter is that the New Testament teachings condemn slavery, condemn racism, condemn all these things . . . the imperialism, abuse of the poor, materialism. It condemns all these things, so I don't feel a contradiction in myself about these things."

"Okay, but what does it say then that the white man's religion is the way? What does that say to African people about their gods, their way of seeing the world, their ideals, the foundations of their culture, man . . . that we need to bow down to this white god? It's not right, Kwabena. It can't be right. I have a real problem with evangelism for that. Okay, then, the white man believes that his way is right; but why can't he keep it to himself? Why should the Yoruba or the Ashanti, or for that matter the Hora, abandon their belief systems for a European one? It's not right, Kwabena. It can't be right."

"But your presumption, Carey, is that one way is the black man's way and the other is the white man's way. But Christianity is as much an imported belief for whites as it is for blacks. The real comparison for the Yoruba or the Ashanti or the Hora would not be the Christians but the Druids. The fact of the matter is that Christianity is not a European religion. It originated in the Middle East, in Asia. In fact Christianity took root in Africa before it did in Europe. And it did not go to Africa at first by force. The Ethiopian Orthodox Church, which is older than any church in Europe, was founded by a eunuch who was christened by St. Paul. So it didn't come to Africa by force. It was there in Ethiopia and Egypt and Sudan before the slave ships—"

"But—"

"No, let me finish. White and black don't work here, Carey. This is not a white man's religion. If you ask me why the belief system of a small Jewish community near Africa has come to have the most relevance to the rest of the world, I would say I don't know. But I would also say I don't feel any racial inadequacy in the face of that truth. In fact, I would like to think that this too could have happened in Wari, Nigeria, or the Yangtze province of China if that had been God's wish. Yes, I can accept that."

"I cannot."

"Why not?"

"Because I think that the worshiping of the white man's god has damaged us. And when I say 'us' I'm not speaking for all of us. Those of us on this side of the Atlantic."

"And the cure for this is for us to find a black religion?"

"I didn't say—"

"In other words, 'Let's have a black religion instead of a

white religion.' That to me is reactionary. And a life of reaction is both limiting and boring. If I accept the premise that there is a universal quest for the truth and that God speaks to all people all over the world, I don't have a problem with a white God, Carey."

I am stunned by this barrage of logic. I don't know what to do. I am defenseless. Still he comes.

"Come on, Carey, name a religion whose believers have upheld its ideals. Buddhism? The Japanese soldiers who overran Asia in the Second World War and forced Korean women to be whores were Buddhist. The men who flew the planes into the World Trade Center were Muslims. The Hindu caste system relegates tens of millions of people to a class known as 'untouchables.' And look at what the Jews have done in Palestine. Carey . . . I cannot tell you what is right for you. I can only tell you what is right for me."

With this he goes inside, his steps shaking the iron floor, causing the ferns on the hooks of the columns to swing a little more in the breeze, braiding their chains. And as I think of how to talk about that other thing between us, he returns with a cereal-colored envelope, addressed to me, in care of him, in a fluttery script that calls to mind the edging on a child's embroidered collar.

I begin to feel a stirring in the depths of me, deeper than flesh, deeper than bone—there, in the plasm, the liquid ooze that glues my life to every life around me, to every microbe, to every virus, to the sperm and egg of every animal that has ever walked this earth.

The letter is from Frances.

In my head I am standing on a boulder by the river that sweeps around the spur of wooded land behind her house. She is wading in the current. Her locks French-braided down her back. Her naked shoulders limp. Her posture mumbling to the world that she has come to a decision that will bring us lots of pain.

Now she is dipping herself in the current to streak her face to hide the water she has sprung herself. And with every dip I start to think that I might lose her, that she will go under and never return, that I won't realize that she has gone until she is already gone, that days will pass until they find her body floating in the foam beneath a waterfall. Then all will have been lost. Nothing will have been gained.

Three weeks ago I was unsure of this, but now, with the arrival of this letter, I know that I am right, and I begin to feel entitled to an audience with all the gods of all the tribes and all peoples of this earth, to ask permission for this love, in turn or in a single oration as passionately persuasive as a hurricane's declaration of its intent to pursue what it believes to be its right of way.

In blues shouts, in jazz riffs, in praise songs—calling out and giving my own response if no one answers.

In haikus, in sonnets, in tautly wrought sestinas, in couplets, in free verse, in the grandiloquent exhortations of Homeric epics, I will plead my case.

I love a woman who does not believe in my God; and I told her that I cannot be with her unless she undergoes baptism. She told me no. I asked her why. She asked me why she should when I did not believe in my God myself. I told her that I did, which made her laugh, which made me shout, which made her laugh some more, which made me tell her all the things Kwabena told me, which made her cry, which made me sneer, which made her shake her head in disbelief, which made me stop and think, which made her curse at me, which made me leave her house.

I stop myself from holding up the letter to the light. Has the envelope been steamed?

Kwabena leans against the back of the chair with loosely folded arms.

"When did it come?"

"Some time last week."

Back in the cottage I allow her words to spurt against my face:

If you were here, in this house, in this kitchen with me, I would boil some eucalyptus tea, and pour it in a mug, and take you to the bedroom, where the lights would be off.

I would take a coil of orange peel, brittle and dry, spark it from the camphor-scented candle by the bed and lay you down on cotton sheets as soft and white as flour.

By orange scent, camphor whiff, and eucalyptus fragrance I would unsheathe you. And you would arch your back and hoist your hips. Complicit.

Beside the bed there would be jars of ointments, secret potions made by cloistered nuns in Axum. And I would rub you, slowly, with Red Sea salts in Blue Nile clay, then lead you to the tub.

The tub would be filled with water. And the water would be sprinkled with bougainvillea petals. And I would place you there before I entered, and pour into the water a quarter gill of the Secret Oil of Atsede the Eritrean, a formulation made of fourteen different tree barks, nineteen different fruits, eighty different nuts, and most importantly, nineteen thousand bud-lettes of a magic tree that flowers twice a century.

I would sing as I administered your ablutions. Then I would lead you to the room again. Place you on the bed again. On your stomach. Pillows piled beneath you.

I would reach into the jars again.

And with closed eyes you will feel my hands hovering over your calves, and you will feel a radiant heat on your skin. When I touch you, you will tingle in four different ways. And you will learn to name the ways in which the four ingredients burn. That burn is cumin. That one is cayenne. That one is mustard seed. That one horseradish. But you will feel no pain, for the coconut oil will soothe you.

I will rub you with this ointment on your legs and on your arms, your muscles turning tender as the spices percolate your pores. And you will feel as if your bones are gone. And you will want to lick your skin. And you will like the taste of you. And you will want to eat yourself. And I will want to eat you, too.

I will reach into another jar . . . and scoop a ridge of butter. And I will reach into some other jars of powders. And in my palm I will make a Three C's unguent according to the recipe of Buzrak, the High Priest of the Court of King Menelik, whose family anointed all the kings of Gonder: cardamom, cinnamon, coriander, cloves.

I would knead this into your bottom. Gather your flesh and press it like dough. Slap it. Poke it. Shape it with my hands. Watch it slowly rising. Marvel as it glimmers in the gloam. Then I would turn you over and wrap you in a shroud of cotton as white as fresh gardenias.

There would be among the jars a tall one. I would open that jar and instruct you to hold it fifteen inches from my breasts, and I would teach you to recite the incantations of the Oracles of Negel, and watch you as you stream into my cleavage a quarter pint of shea-nut oil clotted with gum arabic.

You would smooth it on my nipples and spread it on my breasts. Cream it on my stomach; there, with my index finger, I would trace a Coptic Cross. Then I would get another bottle, which I would hold up to the light.

As you watch I will uncork this bottle. And I will instruct you to tilt it to your head. And you will fill your cheeks. Then you will kneel in front of me, and place your head between my thighs and part your lips inside me. And I will feel the rush. And you will hear the fizz. And I will feel my secret waters beading on my walls. And you will suck these waters out of me.

Then I will ask you to lie down. And with my palms I will close your eyes. And I will lie on top of you. And open my mouth into yours. And I will taste shiraz. And I will taste myself. And you will call my name. And you will smell the room. And you will smell yourself. And you will smell the candle. And you will smell the tea. and you will smell your bath. And you will smell the ointments. And you will smell the or-

*ange peel. And you will smell the wine. And you will smell my
breath in the wine. And you will smell my come on your breath.
And you will come inside me.*

This is what would happen . . . if you were here tonight.

Now it is night. The lights are off. The room is hot. Humid air is
slouching through the open windows. An overhanging branch
begins to scale the roof. The leaves outside are glinting knives,
whittling moonlight into dust. The room is flecked with silver.

Love, I am here, after midnight, alone, curled up on my side,
naked, limp, and wet—shucked from my casing, a ball of tender
flesh. Exposed.

Love, shelter me. Take me in your mouth. Return me to the
sureness of confinement. Bite me. Wet me. Grind me up. Suck
me, love. Drink my juice. Take me far inside your depths. Mix
me with your plasm. Keep me in your blood. Let me be the clot
that never leaves your womb.

Love, you should be here right now, your bottom spooned
against me, your back against my heart, your hand directing
mine to spark the wicks of your congealing breasts. We should
have just returned from eating melons in the kitchen with Nazia
and Kwabena. And the fragrance of the fruit should be enam-
eled on our fingers. And we should have laughed about your
history with Kwabena, and Nazia should have made a joke
about playing spin the bottle, and you should have said you'd
rig it so you'd always get your husband. And I, your husband,
should have caught Kwabena's look of lust.

Love, if you would marry me I would change my occupation.
I would reject the world and be the monk of your religion. I
would study you. Live you. Devote my entire life to you. What
are books compared to you, love? In you there is no beginning,
no middle, no end. Nothing can destroy you. For nothing ex-

isted before you or will live after you. For the world was made from love. In the beginning was the word.

Love, the dampest places on my body are your Eden. Come now. Return. Eat of me. For I am tree. I am grass. I am herb. I am nuts. I am fruit. I am grain. I am bread.

Love, I am a table spread before you. Sup. I am your wine. Your soup. Your tea. Your milk. Your porridge.

CHAPTER TWENTY

The next morning, when I am sure that Kwabena has left for Greeleyville, I go over to the house to use the phone. It is a little after ten and the children are on the veranda dressed for soccer practice—orange shirts, navy shorts, limbs as smooth and brown as sticks of cinnamon.

The eldest one, Adera, is the first to see me. Twelve, with center-parted hair and braces on her teeth, she screams and makes a ragged sprint across the garden path, passing from the glare into the shadow of the overhanging trees, elbows and knees at cross-purposes.

The others follow close behind, shoulders moving side to side, flailing feet turned in.

Nazia is standing at the doorway in a guava-colored frock, her arms above her head, framing her face in a diamond as she ponytails her hair.

In a ring of nasal laughter the children bring me forward, jostling me with all their strength, tugging at my lettuce-colored shirt, clutching my legs through my dark blue jeans.

Swaying with laughter, Nazia reaches over them to greet me with a kiss. A strand of hair comes loose against my face.

"I made you some chapatis," she says, reaching for a dropper on a yellow slatted table stacked with books and magazines: *DoubleTake*, *Newsweek*, *Sports Illustrated*, *ESPN Sports.* The children hoist their chins and gape. She squirts their tongues with vitamins.

"We're off," she says, "to practice. We should be getting back near noon. Can I bring you anything?"

Cudjoe, nine and dark, with his father's chest and nose, says, "Mom, can Uncle Carey come with us?"

Nazia looks at me with smiling eyes. "Well, he might have other things to do."

"But our daddy never comes," says Tano, in a voice too clear for six. "He's always busy."

"Tano, we should never make up stories just to get the things we want."

"Uncle Carey, can you come?" he says, wagging his head of gauzy curls. Like his brother and two sisters, Tano looks Amharic: high round forehead, deep-set eyes, broad cheekbones and a jawline made of curves instead of angles.

"Tomorrow might be better," I tell him as I think of calling Frances.

"Will you juggle the balls like you did in that picture?"

I say yes although I don't recall the shot, then watch from the veranda till they leave. After which I dial Frances's number.

What will I say? I'm not sure. In the past I would have known. But everything is different now. I've changed. No, I'm taking too much credit. She has changed me.

When the phone begins to ring I cannot think beyond "Hello." Too nervous to tremble, I can only stand still.

It is ringing. It is ringing. Pick up. Pick up. After three or four rings there is a hitch and a pause, and I set my jaws and lips to say hello but no one answers. Instead I hear a set of beeps arranged in rising pitch; then there is a message: "Since you did not select a carrier, this call cannot be completed at this time. . . ."

There is more. But I cannot bear to listen. There is no long distance service here. I need a phone card or a mobile.

The telephone is mounted on the wall above an L-shaped row of cupboards. The sink is in the joint. The cupboard doors have panes of frosted glass. The pulls are made of brass.

Below an upper cupboard filled with custard-colored crockery is a basket on a counter laid with blue ceramic tiles. There are papers in the basket, credit-card bills, a letter from a gym, junk mail, a grocery list.

A vein begins to wriggle at my temple. Does the basket look as if it has been riffled? I pull a drawer out enough to sift it with a shake. Nothing, still. If I had a car I would drive to the store. Maybe I should rent one. Maybe they'd deliver.

I lean against the counter. I don't know what to do. There is no bus here that I know of.

There has to be another telephone. The line would be the same. Perhaps it could be different. Upstairs in the bedroom? The living room perhaps.

My lungs are heavy as I climb the stairs. What if there is someone here? I take my time, measuring my shoes against the steps. One hand on the balustrade.

From the landing I can see Kwabena's door. It is open. Through the oval frame I see a detail of his room: sisal mat, light blue sheets, a trunk bed, a heavy dresser crammed with books and paper, simple cotton panties on a Windsor chair. High cut. Black. Ripped and flung perhaps.

But as I pause to ask myself if I can do this, and as my need to speak to Frances tells me that I can, I hear the buzz of voices. Nazia and the children have returned.

I am seated in the kitchen by the time they reach the house, dipping a chapati in a bowl of channa dal.

"He left a shin pad," Nazia says as Tano capers up the steps.

"Uncle Carey, are you coming?"

"Are you sure you don't want to come?"

Nazia shakes her head, charmed by her son's insistence. I have no choice. I have to go.

When I exit Nazia's Taurus at the fields on Polo Road, Tano drags me off to meet his coach, a man with a skinny neck that flies a flag of skin. There are perhaps a dozen pitches here. Each one has its little pair of bleachers where the children and their parents shade themselves beneath umbrellas.

The fields are in a bowl. Around us an embankment rises in a rug of scrub and dandelions to a ridge of evergreens.

The grass is green in patches, but like Kwabena's neighbors mostly everyone is white—middle class to wealthy from the vehicles in the parking lot: European four-doors and domestic SUVs.

"So," Nazia says when she comes to sit with me. "Is there anything you want to get besides a mobile phone?"

"Maybe a car," I say. "I don't want to tie you up in case you need to go somewhere. It's summer. You must have lots of things to do. The kids are out of school."

"Okay. I need to watch the kids so—"

"I understand." I pat her hand. "I understand."

"I am sorry for being so hard on you. I have been just as hard on my husband."

"Never mind."

She gloves her hand in mine and says, while looking at the game: "We'll go when we are finished."

On the field, Tano gets the ball and Nazia starts to scream: "Run, Tano, run!"

He runs into a crowd.

"Isn't he brave," his mother chimes, "to try to take them on like that?"

"Change his name to Mel. Call him Braveheart."

She bounces me with her shoulder.

"Were you brave like that?" she asks.

I cannot answer. All these children. All these parents. All this pride. This is something I have never known.

When we moved to Kingston, my mother enrolled us at a Jewish school, Hillel. On the Sabbath she took us to the synagogue. After school, three times a week, we would go with her to the sugar estates to teach first aid and Spanish and that is how I learned to play—from pickup games with older boys who had learned to play from men.

I asked my mother for soccer boots when I was fourteen years old. She told me no. As a communist she thought it would be decadent. Didn't I already have a pair of sneakers?

When I asked my father he took me to the lawn and pointed to the houses all around me. These people, he told me, play tennis, and I already had a pair of tennis shoes. Soccer, like reggae, was for hooligans. Soccer boots? Not with his money. Not with his blood and perspiration.

I had never seen my father go to work.

I bought the boots myself. I bought a book of magic tricks and learned to cheat at cards; then I began to gamble with the men on the estate. And when I had enough I bought my boots.

I lied to my mother. I told her I had won a gift certificate to Sports & Games. At first she did not believe me, but my brother lied to help me, and unlike me he was known to always speak the truth.

I was wearing the boots, juggling a ball in the living room as my mother and sisters watched, when my father opened the door. My brother had gone to study on the veranda.

My father stood in the doorway with his hands in his pockets, watching without saying a word.

"What kind are they?" he asked eventually.

"A Puma King Pele," I replied. I held the ball in the crook of my arm.

"I love the smell of new leather," he said. "It reminds me of a new car. Take them off and let me smell them."

I glanced at my mother. She nodded. I handed my father the boots.

He held them to his face and inhaled deeply, then looked at me and smiled. "Here, see what I mean."

Tricked, I leaned into the blow. He had swung the cleats across my face.

I turned around to glance at my mother. She was cuddling my sisters, who were screaming.

"Didn't I tell you no?" my father asked. His voice was insistent but reasoned.

"But I bought them with my own money."

"Do you work?"

"No, Daddy."

"Where did you get it?"

I pointed.

"From Mummy."

My mother and my sisters looked away.

"Look at me," my father said. I obeyed him. "There is only one man in this house."

I shook my head and turned and walked away. He ordered me to stop. I did not listen.

I walked toward the gate with my swollen face and sat beneath an orange tree and tried to cry, tried so hard to cry, because I thought it was the natural thing to do.

My father strolled outside. In one hand was a machete and a bucket. In the other hand my boots.

He looked at me. I looked at him. Our eyes locked. In my head I heard a click as they loaded. And I watched my father place my boots beneath the bucket that we used to kill the Sunday chicken, leaving out the tips.

He chopped one and then the other, sauntered to the gate and threw the tipless boots out in the street. A car went by and flattened them. A dog began to sniff them, grabbed one in his mouth and ran away.

I closed my eyes and tried to understand my father's wicked ways. I could not. Then I tried to understand my lack of rage. How does one hate without anger?

As I searched my soul for answers there came rising up inside me the musings of a rastaman, explaining in a reasoned voice the simple dialectic of cathartic revolution.

I shot the sheriff.

When I went to see my mother in Tel Aviv two weeks ago, she did not remember this story. She does not remember many things these days. I had not seen her in almost seven years. She has changed a lot. Now she is an Orthodox Jew. She lives with a lesbian lover. The woman is forty-two; mother is sixty-six. Her mind is lively but unfocused. She speaks with passion about the smallest things . . . a flower or a shoe.

Sometimes an old memory becomes a new one and she cannot tell the difference. She remembers Cuba better than she does New York. Sometimes she thinks that her lover is her nurse. Sometimes she shocks the nurse by caressing her like her lover.

Her lover, who was born in Ethiopia, confided that they are not lovers anymore and that she used to be her nurse. The lover used me to fill in some of the gaps in their lives. What was my mother like? Who were her friends? What is the meaning of the word *chinloy*?

My explanation makes her laugh. My mother utters *chinloy* when she comes. The lover thought it was a Jamaican term of endearment. I didn't mention that I had caught her and the neighbor in bed or that he was not her only affair. Although she does not remember me, she is, after all, my mother.

I stayed in Israel for a week. When I left my mother called me by the gardener's name. She asked me for my father. I told her that he had died. I did not remind her that she had gone to the funeral or that I had stayed away, or that he had come to see me at the Public Theater the week before he passed away, or that our meeting had ended with violence, or that I believed deep down inside myself that I was responsible for his death because as his son I should have found a way to take care of him in his old age, or that I know if I had found a way to save him then he would not have been sleeping on the sidewalk that night when those young boys with nothing to do decided to rob him, or that he had tried to fight them all, all five of them, or that he broke the jaws of three of them, or that they eventually overpowered him and stomped him to death.

I did not tell her these things. Neither did I tell her that I was so consumed with guilt that I tried to kill myself, nor that I drove from New York to South Carolina, nor that I almost made it.

"Carey. Carey." Nazia is tapping my shoulder. "Are you okay?"

She is standing. I am sitting. I reach out to embrace her. And my arm finds its way around her waist.

"You are a good mother, Nazia."

She smiles and leans against me. A little bit unsure of what to do, she sits and drapes my arm around her shoulder. I pull away. She will harass me if she smells my cigarettes.

"When are you leaving?" she asks, gesturing with a bangled wrist.

"I don't know. A week. Some days. Two weeks."

"I need you to do me a favor. Kwabena is into basketball but the children prefer soccer. Will you coach them for me? I think they have some talent, but I don't think I understand the game."

A parent calls out from the turf below. I follow Nazia's gaze beyond the rail and see, clipped to the woman's pocket, a silver mobile phone.

I wrap my locks into a turban.

"Nazia," I whisper. "I will coach the kids if you ask that woman to let me use her phone."

She whips around.

"Are you serious?"

"As a judge."

Cocking her arms to balance herself, she takes the steps in twos, sunlight burning through her dress, throwing her form in silhouette, the narrow waist, the gentle hips, the pouch between her thighs.

I make myself unsee her as she floats along the touchline, weaving through great herds of grazing parents.

When she finds the woman there is pointing, laughter, the shaking of heads; then, as my chest begins to tighten and my nose begins to bead with sweat, Nazia turns to me and makes a quick salute.

"Are you calling Kwabena?" she asks when she returns.

The question is innocent, nonetheless a nuisance.

"Yes."

She is standing close to me. I turn away from her to shield the numbers. The beeps are soft. She cannot count the digits.

Keeping my back to her and pointing to my ear as I excuse myself, I cross the aisle to get some space. My shirt is wet and draping like a sleeping infant.

Eight rings. Nine rings.

"Hello."

It is the helper.

"Hi, Claudette, this is Carey. How are you? Is Miss Frances there?"

"No, sir."

"Would you—"

She cuts me off.

"Is not really my prerogative, sir, but you shouldn't do her the way you do her, sir. I don't like to see advantage taken, sir. And what you do to Miss Frances was not right, sir. People have to learn to live loving, sir. And you can't just walk away from a person that way, sir. People have to learn to hold hand and one person say to the other one, 'Come, darling,' sir. The two of you is two intelligent people, sir. It shouldn't really come to that."

I don't know what to say.

"You have nothing to say for yourself, sir? Is so you brazen, sir? Is so you bare-faced, sir? Is so you bumptious, bright, and bold, sir?"

"No, Claudette. It is nothing like that. I'm at a football game. I can't really talk right now."

"Why you cause her so much heartache, Mr. Carey?"

"Claudette—"

"You have a heart."

Over my shoulder Nazia is watching Tano with her fingers clasped with joy.

"Claudette, I have to go. I'm using someone's phone. Where can I reach Frances? We have to speak."

"She gone Africa, sir."

I clap my hand to my forehead.

"What?"

"Yes, sir. Miss Frances was waiting to hear from you. But she gone Africa last week."

"When is she coming back?"

"I don't know, sir."

"What do you mean?"

"So I buy it, so I sell it. I don't add on any profit."

CHAPTER TWENTY-ONE

From Kwabena's house to the cottage the land is flat and grassy, then it rises in a steady grade of sycamore, pine, and walnut to a simple wooden fence; there it billows steeply.

At the top of the hill is a bearded oak, and there in its shade, on a swing, as Kwabena's grandparents must have done in their time, I sit in the evenings to gaze across the railway cut, toward the worn-out houses lining Millwood Street, the crumbs and remnants of the negro town devoured by the city.

The little gabled houses, which are raised on small pylons, are of brick. So closely are they set against the road that it is possible to spit frustrations from the porch into the window of a passing car.

How different life would be if we could do that? Just hack it up and spit it out and clog up someone else's life?

On the evenings when I'm feeling most reflective I will choose a passing car and follow it with my gaze beyond the worn-out houses and the mangy supermarket and the aisle of greasy restaurants.

I always place a couple in the car. A man and woman in love.

Sometimes I give them names. Simple names like Mary and Joe. They are always holding hands.

Or sometimes Joe has his hand on Mary's leg. Mary's leg is always firm but damp with perspiration. And if Mary is pregnant, as she sometimes is, Joe will rub her tummy through her dress. And Mary will feel in Joseph's touch an owning of the carnal thought that fattened her. And he always tells her that her flesh is his delight, a thing of beauty to be wanted and consumed, a treat, an indulgence—a confection wet with eggs and butter.

In the car there is always music. Reggae or rhythm and blues. If it's R&B it's always music by a righteous singer. Stevie Wonder. Marvin Gaye. Curtis Mayfield. Isaac Hayes. If it's reggae then it's always by a lover man. Gregory Isaacs. Delroy Wilson. Dennis Brown.

And Joe and Mary always know the songs. And they are always singing out of tune. And there is always a moment when they are so taken by the song, so filled up with the song that they begin to find the notes that chart the song, and they begin to use the song to map their love.

Sometimes they will imagine their love as a song, the living lyrics of a song of great emotion—a Gershwin song, a Marley song, a Paul McCartney song.

Sometimes they will imagine their love as a painting and ask themselves is this a Picasso love or a Reubens love? A Clemente or a Bearden love?

Sometimes Joe will tell Mary that their love is not a painting but a poem. And she will say by Browning. And he will say by Brooks. And she will say by Marvell. And he will say by Walcott. And she will say by Hughes. And he will say Guillén. And she will say Rilke. And he will say Cortéz. And she will say Césaire. And he will say Neruda. Then they will chorus, "I wish."

This has now become my Césaire Guillén ritual. In the evenings, when the sun begins to flare like a sodium flash and the scene below me fades to sepia, I call Frances on my mobile phone. Claudette says there is nothing new. She hangs up. I call again. She scolds me. I take it. I cry.

In the mornings I drive my rented Jeep to Polo Road. I run. By seven I am home writing. By nine I have the kids paired off for passing drills. By ten I take them down to practice.

From noon until Kwabena comes—twoish in the afternoon— I sort out my affairs. . . . The contractor who is renovating my basement has discovered signs of termites. . . . A producer in Toronto needs to hear a yes or no. . . . My quarterly taxes are overdue. . . . Zadie's mother is ill and so she needs time off to go to California. . . . There are readings to schedule. . . . lectures to give . . . life is going on.

At night Kwabena comes to meet me here beneath the oak tree and we talk about the only thing there is to talk about. It is therapeutic but unpleasant.

We have been meeting for twelve nights now. At first it was hard. As a Christian, Kwabena has a commitment to truth. And there are times when I wish he would lie. If he lies to me and I unearth the lie I will be on equal footing. Kwabena challenges many of the things that I relate. He prods me, dismisses me, accuses me of bending the truth to protect her name. Sometimes he will stare at me blankly, daring me to convince him that I have left nothing out.

But I believe everything he tells me.

"You have to really know her parents to understand her," he tells me one night. "Her mother was married twice before she met her father. And it was strongly rumored that her father was abusing her."

I am sitting on the swing and he is standing.

"People say a lot of things about a lot of people," I defend.

"No. Trust me. This is fact. That is why she was acting up and had to be sent to live with us." He begins to shift his weight from leg to leg now. "Auntie Margaret, her mother, just didn't understand. They did all sorts of things with her. They sent her to psychologists. They are Catholics, so Auntie Margaret sent her to a priest."

"A priest for what?"

"To be exorcised. It was a really bad situation. As a child sometimes she would come over to our house and just destroy my sister's toys. One time she ran away. She used to steal things. You had to lock things up whenever she was around."

"So do you think she was abused?"

"I strongly suspect it."

"But do you know for a fact?" I ask directly.

"Are you asking me if she told me?"

I was not, but his question gives me an idea.

"Yes, that is what I am asking."

"No. She did not. But I heard it from my father. I heard him say that her father did things that would have gotten him arrested in America."

I lose my patience.

"But that could be anything."

"Come on, Carey, you can see the way she relates to men and know that something screwy went on!"

"I thought I knew you better."

"What?"

"So if a woman has a healthy appetite it means she was abused?"

"Her appetite is more than healthy, Carey. She believes that the world of sex is an all-you-can-eat buffet."

"Who are you to judge?" I shout.

"I am not standing in judgment," he says calmly. "In all the years that we have known each other, have I ever judged you?"

He opens his palm. His eyes are soft. I think of all the times that I have turned to him for help.

"No, Kwabena. You have not."

He puts his hand on my shoulder.

"So why are you doubting me now?"

"I am not doubting you," I say weakly.

"Why do you come to me when you are in trouble?" He does not wait for me to answer. "Because you know that you can trust me. Because you know that I understand you. Because you know that anything you tell me will stay with me. Because you know that I have never wavered from the things that I believe."

"I fell in love with her, Kwabena."

He pauses. He glances at his feet, perhaps to hide his eyes, and takes me by both shoulders.

"Try to understand that I fell in love with her as well, and she broke my heart," he pleads. "If I overstepped my bounds, if I said things that made you disappointed in me, if I showed the nasty, dirty side that all humans have, it is because I don't want her to break your heart as well. Carey, I have seen you at your lowest. I have seen what can happen to you when your heart is broken. Your father broke your heart, Carey. Your father gave you hope that perhaps you two could share the kind of love that a father and son should have and then he went away and got himself killed because of false pride and you took it so hard. I saw you bloodied and disoriented. I called the police. I called the ambulance. I spoke to my wife and told her that we should ask you to stay with us when you got out of the hospital because I didn't think it was a good idea for you to go back to New York alone. I love you, man. I love you. And because I love you, Carey, and because I know what lies in store for you, and because I know what you have been through, I made a hard decision. I could stand aside as I have always done in the past, or I could step in, knowing that if I stepped in I would have to step in in a dramatic way, and that this might cause you to hate me. But I would rather you hate me, Carey, I would rather suffer that hurt, than to have you love me and end up being hurt by that woman in ways I can do nothing about. This is not about my feelings for her. This is about my feelings for you."

As he studies me I concentrate on not blinking. If I do I will cry. There is nothing wrong with crying, or with crying in front of him. But crying will distract me and I need to bring my thoughts to bear to ask a crucial question.

"That time," I begin, "that time at your house. I have been meaning to ask you. Why were you watching her on TV?"

He pulls away and crosses his arms, then covers his mouth with an open hand and begins to tap his nose, marking time, counting down the moments to his answer. In the dark it is hard to read his expression. Perhaps he is disappointed. Perhaps I did not thank him for his support over the years or explain to him that now that he has explained himself I understand and appreciate his intervention.

"I need you to forgive me," he says weakly.

I stand and walk toward him. He backs away.

"Kwabena."

"No, Carey."

"Kwabena."

He stops and piles his hands atop his head.

"I told you a lie."

"Don't fuck with me."

"I did."

"What? When?"

"She was not abused. I made it up."

I realize that I have not been breathing when a long, wet sigh seeps out of me.

I tilt my head to call him. With his head turned down he comes to me. I take two steps to meet him. Now he is standing close enough for me taste his breath. A vein begins to branch across his forehead.

"Why the fuck would you do that?"

"To keep you away from her."

"I thought she didn't matter."

"She does. Of course she does."

"She matters after all this time?"

"Well, life is funny that way."

I turn away from him.

"Does Nazia know?"

"She doesn't. But it's harmless."

"And I'm not going to say anything."

"That is neither here nor there."

"What are we going to do, Kwabena?"

"I will continue to do what I have done," he says as he makes his way down the hill toward the house. "I will manage this love like a chronic illness that flares up every now and then."

"And what if we get together?"

He stops and turns around.

"What are the likely chances of that?"

"You don't have to sound that way."

"What way?"

"As if it's the end of the world and you can say all the fucked-up things you have ever wanted to say to me."

"You are reading into things, Carey. I didn't mean to sound any way. I am just a tired black man who needs to go and lie down with his wife. She is all I have in the world right now."

"So you're just going to leave me up here like this."

"There is a lot for you to work out, my friend."

"I am not feeling like you're my friend right now."

"Carey," he says, "I kept a letter from her until you arrived. I could have read it. I could have destroyed it. But I did not."

"I'm sorry," I call out as he fades into the forest.

"When she gets into your blood," he cautions, "she doesn't go away."

I cup my hands to my mouth.

"What are we going to do?"

"Worry about yourself. I have my wife. I have my children. I have God. I will manage."

"Fuck," I admit. "I have nothing."

I have nothing but memories and dreams. And this night, as I have done on many nights, I go to bed and think about the house in Elder River.

I saw the house before we left the gravel road that led us from the Junction Road into the town.

The sun was setting, but the air was still warm, and people sheltered lazily beneath their bright umbrellas or dabbed themselves with handkerchiefs or wiped themselves with rags.

As we passed the market and were swiftly changing lanes, a yellow kite came drifting into view, maybe twenty feet above the ground.

I traced the string and saw a little girl elated by the joy of flight, letting out her paper bird, then jerking it to make it climb, trying to catch a current, guided by a man whom I presumed to be her father.

He instructed her by holding an imaginary string, smiling broadly like a wedge of honeydew.

I began to think about the fact that I had never flown a kite. Who would have taught me? My mother? She was too busy with her affairs and convictions. My father? He was too busy refining embarrassing ways to hurt himself and those around him.

As I considered these things I saw the house in the distance, near the apex of a hill, a yellow house that stood without the company of neighbors.

I thought about the house again some fifteen minutes later when we pulled up at the gate.

I had closed my eyes to shut out Frances Carey, experiencing the balance of the journey as a code of shifting gears.

When I looked again she was standing at the gate, an elbow

resting on a concrete column, which was painted white and finished with a row of lattice blocks with yellow crotons poking through.

The crotons were taller than the height of a man. But taller than the crotons were the bushy bougainvilleas, their slender arcing branches weighted down with tiny fuchsia flowers, and above the bougainvilleas was the afroed mango tree.

"Are you coming in?" she asked.

"Yes."

She bit her upper lip and held it as she swung her arms, twitching muscles flexing through her skin.

"Are you coming in?" she asked again.

"I said yes."

"It will be very hard to do that if you're sitting in the car."

"I will get out in my own time."

"Is that the same thing as when you're ready?"

"Nothing as childish as that."

She looked away. The tendons in her neck began to rise.

"There is no reason to be ugly, Carey."

"Truth is not always pretty."

A moth began to wander in a circle near her face. She jerked her head and fanned it with her palm, settling down to glare at me, my face, but not my eyes, at a spot between my knitted brows.

"Life isn't always pretty, Carey. As a writer you should know that."

"It isn't always pretty," I replied, "but that doesn't mean you have to go out chasing ugly things."

"But what about the ugly things inside you? Those are always with you while you run from other things."

"Please, don't analyze me."

"I am not trying to analyze you."

She began to twist a croton leaf.

"Oh, I am sorry," I muttered. "You are being wise."

"And I take it you are being stupid."

"I draw the line at 'stupid,' Frances. Do not call me stupid."

She reached along the leaf and broke a twig. The bush went whipping back. A flock of pink and yellow butterflies erupted.

"Okay, I won't call you stupid, Carey. What should I call you?"

"A cab."

"So you are not coming in."

"Just call me a cab."

"And where should I say you are going?"

"That is my concern."

"On my telephone it is my concern as well."

"I used to have a telephone."

"I will buy you a replacement."

"That won't be necessary."

"But calling you a cab is? Is that something you have to do each day like masturbate and take a shit?"

"You can be so gross."

"Aren't you the man who was ready to flash his cock at me after knowing me a minute?"

"That is so ridiculous."

"So it was closer to an hour—but the fact is that—"

"You are gross."

"And what are you, Carey?"

"I don't want to go there with you."

"Go there. Please lead me. I will follow."

"If there is one thing I want to tell you though it's this: You won't have to worry about going anywhere with me again."

"But where have we gone together, Carey? Bed?"

"A familiar destination, I have gathered."

"Familiar to who?"

"To all the men that you have gone with."

"What can I say? My hole is unforgettable. But what's the point? That you can't just fuck me and forget me the way you always do?"

"You don't know a thing about me. So you can say whatever you want."

"I take freedom of speech for granted."

"Say what you want, okay. Just don't say it to Carey."

"So now you're referring to your other self. Which self do I have in front of me now? Where did Carey go? Listen . . . whoever you are . . . Mr. Carey's evil twin. In Mr. Carey's absence, who should I say my little thingys to?"

"To yourself."

"And if I want to speak aloud?"

A vein began to wriggle down her forehead. Her brows were drawn. Her jaws were set. Her lids were angled louver blades. She was ready to fight and I was not. If she continued, I accepted, I could grab her.

"Frances, why are you trying to start an argument?"

"Mr. Wise Potato Chip, I am sorry that you are late, but the argument has already started. You are so slow. And when I call you stupid then you take offense."

"Fuck you."

"Which is really what you want to do."

"You are mad."

She took a step toward me, her elbows bent, her fingers forming fists.

"But isn't it true? Isn't that what you really want to do right now?"

She flashed her hands and spun around. Her sandals slipped, then anchored, crunching grains of dirt into the tar.

How did I get to this? I covered my face in my hands and shook my head. How could all this happen in a day? How could she matter so much so quickly? Why did I feel a need to stay and work this out? And how did she know?

The dull ache on my leg was now an intermittent pulse. How did she know before me? Was it my eyes? My voice? Had I been twirling my hair?

She crossed her ankles, closed herself off, placed her hands behind her and pulled her shoulders back, causing her breasts to rise behind the knotted blouse, then jiggle as she slipped her weight from hip to hip.

A film of sweat appeared between the *lappa* and the blouse.

"You want to fuck me, don't you, Carey? I know you do. But you may not even know it. In your head you just want to shut me up. And you are trying to find the way to do it. But there is a part of you that wants to use your wit to numb me. But you know that that won't work. Not with me at least, for I am just as smart as you." She pointed with an open hand. "Who do you think you are? Some kind of isolated genius? The more I talk, Carey, the angrier you will get, until the truth of what you want to do begins to prick your brain. But the truth won't come like that. Your ego is too big, so it will come another way. It will come as an urge to grab me. Yes, but if you grab me, Carey, I will resist. And if you keep on grabbing me I will fight. I will say things that will make you bitter. I will tell you things about yourself. About you and your father. And your mother. And the little rotten pussy girls you like to fuck. I will push you till you slap me. And as you slap me I will scratch you. And I will keep on scratching you. And you will keep on slapping me, thinking that another slap is all that it will take to shut me up. But mark my words, you will be sorry if you do that. Because I will fight you like a man. And as we tussle you will see my nostrils flare. And you will see the pumping veins along my neck. And you will hear me grunting in your ear. And as you wrestle me you will tear my blouse to hold me back from punching you. And you will see my breasts hang down. And when you see your nail marks on the fucking breasts that gave you comfort, negro, you will feel so fucking bad. And you will hate yourself. And you know why you will hate yourself? You will hate yourself because you allowed your stupid fucking ego to lead you to a head space where you are beating down your woman by her gate. And that is when you will really want to fuck me bad, because your ego will tell you that you are fucking me just to sweet me up so I won't call the rass police or pay a shotter boy to done your life. You will think that. You will think that. You will think that. And this is the truth right here: that you are not man enough to manage me. If you were any kinda man, Carey, I wouldn't be talking to you like this. We wouldn't be arguing right now. You would be commanding me to repair to my room and prepare myself to receive you. And you know that I would go. And you know that I would take the time to bathe and put on something nice and when I get the loving deep inside me I'm going to whisper, 'Daddy, I am sorry. I am such a miserable woman. Please don't leave me. Please.' "

My head began to tremble. I got out of the car and walked toward the bush, which started just beyond the middle of the road. The road was crumbling, returning to a former life as gravel. This is my fucking life, I thought. Eroded. Soon I'll be no more. The bush has come to claim me.

I stood on the edge of the precipice and watched the land descending smoothly to the town and saw the gravel road that we had taken.

On the floor of my attention something fluttered. It was the kite. The string had broken. It was floating in a stream of wind, unmoored.

And once again I thought about my father, about our early disconnection. I also thought about the father with the little girl. In my head I saw him holding her and promising to build a better kite for her tomorrow and teaching her a lesson: that the wind will take our things unless we hold them tightly.

Frances interrupted me.

"Don't believe the voices in your head. You cannot fly."

I replied without looking: "You are not as funny as you think."

"I don't think I am funny at all. Right now I just feel pathetic."

"You are not alone."

Don't look, I thought. Don't look.

"So you are feeling pathetic, too?" she asked.

"I don't have words to waste."

"Is that a yes?"

"It's a no. Take it as a no. There are many more pathetic people like you in the world . . . people who don't live their lives as much as they construct them from the shards of adolescence. That is where they break you." I was thinking of my father and the soccer boots. "Adolescence. That period when you try to make your place in history by being something different. If you are lucky you will get over it. If not, you end up being you."

"Don't look now," she said. "I'm crying."

"You'll make me cry as well. Don't do that."

"What do you have to cry about?"

"Pathetic people like you?"

"And what do you do for people like yourself?"

"There is nothing to be done for people like me but administer last rites and read a pleasant eulogy. People like me are not pathetic, love. We are tragic."

"Don't look, okay. Promise me you won't."

"I already said I wouldn't."

"Don't. Because I am laughing as I am crying and I get really ugly then, and I want you to fall in love with me all over again when you turn around to look at me."

"I will never turn around to look at you. There is something in the legend of Medusa that is clawing at my brain."

"So you think I'm truly ugly."

"You are beyond beautiful."

"Do you love me, Carey?"

I closed my eyes and heard her sandals softly crunching on the asphalt, then the coolness of her shadow, then her smell, an odor that was subtle but enduring, like the smell of green tomatoes.

My hands sought refuge in my pockets. Her arms encircled me. Against my back I felt the hardness of her nipples, the softness of her breasts, then her body damp and languid.

With her breathing steaming through my shirt, a hand began to tug my belt.

The hand began to search inside, touching things, petting things—holding, stroking, pumping. I turned and she squatted. Behind her was the car, behind the car the gate, behind the gate the house. And right there, as the sun began to melt, her face became a mold of streaming wax.

As we leaned against the car she said: "I know that we will work this out."

The lights were on in the town below. The temperature had fallen and a wind had begun to shake the trees. In the darkness shadows would congeal to form the outline of a man—a tree trunk, some branches, a head comprised of fruit and leaves— and at times I felt uneasy. Sometimes a firefly would flame and disappear, its spurting color reabsorbed into the thickness like a stubbed cigarette.

"We have a lot to talk about," I told her. "A lot to talk about."

The shirt with which I'd wiped her face was crusting in my hands.

"Not just to talk about," she added. "To work out as well."

"Yeah. To work out. There are a lot of things to work out. So many things to work out."

I closed my eyes. I felt her turn her head to place her other cheek against my chest and heard the crackle as our skins began to peel away. With her cooler cheek against my face she held her breath and said: "Tell me, don't try to spare my feelings. Do you love me?"

"If I didn't love you I'd be gone somewhere. I don't know where. But away from here."

"Will you give me the same answer when I ask you in the morning?"

"I will."

"And will I be able to feel this love? Like, will I be able to look at you and say: 'This negro loves me?' Will I just know it the way that Graça Machel looks at Nelson Mandela and just knows?"

"Graça and Nelson. That is a very great love."

"She was married to his friend and comrade, Samora Machel. That did not matter in the end."

"I know what you are saying. But this is not the same."

"I know it's not the same. But can you see what I am saying?"

"I do. But Mandela is a greater man than most of us—than me."

"I know what you are saying. And I love Mandela, too. But next to me, in my house, Carey, no man is greater than you."

CHAPTER TWENTY-TWO

What I thought had been the house was not the house. What I thought had been the gate was not the gate. The yellow house was in fact the yellow office.

The house in which she lived was white and royal blue. The entrance was a quarter-mile along the road, which curled around a wooded spur.

It was an old house, built into the hill on a ledge below the point at which the gradient tumbled steeply to the river.

The lower floor was made of stone, the upper floor of wood. But so steep was the slope and so narrow was the ledge that I could see only the roof as I approached.

A row of peaks with missing shingles, the roof was overhung by old-growth trees, some of which shot upward from the riverbank below.

The house had been constructed as an inn, but on the upper floor where Frances slept the walls had been removed to make a long and narrow lofty space with honey-colored floors.

To reaffirm it as a single space, Frances had replaced the doors that faced the mountain with a giant set of louver-bladed win-

SATISFY MY SOUL ● 169

dows. The walls were white. The trim was blue. Descending through the rafters was a row of wooden ceiling fans, some of which had missing blades.

There were no dividing walls but there was an order to the place. At one end was the bedroom. The middle was the lounge and kitchenette. At the far end was the library, the racks for her guitars, and the easel where she painted landscapes and portraits in caffeinated colors.

I awoke the next morning to the rushing of the river. My chest was curled around her shoulder blades. She was sleeping with a fist against her mouth.

It was a large bed, old, with a trunk, and the headboard was low with spiral posters. It was hard to leave her there.

From my bag at the foot of the bed beside a wicker rocking chair I took a purple guayabera, shook it out, slipped it on, and went out on the terrace with one of her guitars.

The terrace was not a terrace. It was in fact a deck, a deck that stretched about a hundred feet with tree-wells in the planking—holes through which the ancient trees erupted to the sky: vanilla, eucalyptus, sycamore, mahoe, and flame of the forest.

There were chairs among the tree trunks, some arranged with tables, a hammock, a tubular chaise with yellow canvas strapping, painted tires filled with flowers.

In one corner by the railing was a partly rusted glider, and I sat there with my elbows on my knees, the body of the Gibson resting on my feet, my hands around the neck.

Gazing down the bank toward the river, which was narrow and swift and olive from the shadow of the overhanging trees, and white where it tumbled over rocks, I admitted to myself that I could live here.

I played for a while, aimlessly, my mind drifting from Poonks and Papa Bear to Rozette to Kwabena, to the kite, to the argument, to the mystery of our meeting, to the climb toward the spirit from the belly of the cave.

After that there was the falling and the recognition, the understanding that I had nothing there to catch me, nothing as reliable as faith.

The river made me thirsty and I went inside, passing from the shade into the heat then back into the shade of the overhanging roof, which was supported by a line of wooden columns.

Frances was lying on her back, her arms at her side, her legs straight ahead of her, her knees slightly bent, her hair fanned out against the pillow, which was orange like the rumpled sheets.

Last night I had held her in my arms until she cried herself to sleep. We did not make love. Instead we talked, talked about everything except us—mainly about politics and business—and in this way came to know each other better; and it occurred to me how much personal facts can be distracting, that how you think is more relevant and revealing than what you say.

Frances and I reason differently. For Frances there is nothing contradictory about a contradiction. She believes in women's rights but would not hire an expectant mother. She hates communism but reveres Fidel Castro. She disagrees with capital punishment: The state should not kill murderers, but it must because most murderers are not honorable enough to volunteer to kill themselves.

She has a familiar kind of brilliance, that of the young writer who does not take the time to edit, who shares the work before it's ready, the kind of writer who, driven by passion and intuition, creates the kind of work that shatters paradigms, that changes the way we see the world.

For Frances Carey, I discovered, a contradiction is a countermelody. For me it is a jarring note. Discovering this difference both charmed and frightened me. For in it I saw a vision of my younger self, the self I had outgrown.

Was I better then? Or am I better now? Six of one. Half a dozen of the other. Different and the same.

As I watched her stirring in her sleep, I thought about the awkwardness the night before. During our conversation, she had begun to stroke my stomach in the dark, her wrist shaking, her fingers tense.

I lay without moving as she took her time, parting and un-coiling my pubic hairs, pulling, holding, then letting go, circling my cock, which just lay there, neither tired nor aloof, but re-laxed and introspective like a yogi.

"Do you want me?" she asked.

"I don't know," I told her. "Maybe you should ask me in the morning."

Now the sun had risen.

With a glass of water I went to the library and took a seat at the table, which was long and wide and covered to the floor with a length of tasseled velvet that was black with golden bor-ders. Around the table there were sixteen chairs, all of them dif-ferent, none of them new—office chairs, kitchen chairs and various kinds of stools, some in wood, some in steel, one in plastic and Formica.

She had as many books as I had. But none of them were shelved. They were simply piled against the wall like bricks, completely covering the shorter wall, extending down the longer wall for maybe twenty feet.

In the shutter-slatted dimness, I sat down in a button-tufted chair that made me feel the urge to write. But I did not want to write, because I thought that I would write only of sadness.

I shifted to a stool and took a pencil from a mug. Perhaps I would draw. I tore a leaf from a book and drew a line, but the line became a letter and I began to write, and the writing came smoothly and steadily, then erupted like a wave that hits a hid-den reef.

My pencil waded through the words toward that hidden

thing. It dove below the surface, where it led me to a memory of a place.

In a watery trance where every object was a shadow flecked with light, I saw below me, floating in a gun-gray current the bones of dead Africans in schools like fish, each bone moving according to the rhythm of its tribe, Fanti bones, Ibo bones, Mandingo bones, Coromantee bones, Malinke bones, Ashanti bones, then bones no more, just ribbons of chains snaking past like silver eels, miles and miles of chains, chains for hands, chains for feet, chains for the waists of pregnant women, chains for the necks of infants, then the anchor chain and the hook, then the sunken ships as big as whales, and for the first time in my life I was drawn into that vision of another life without passing through the threshold of sleep.

With my eyes open but narrowed in concentration, I heard a chorus singing in a language that I have always known without knowing, sweet songs of lamentation for a boy named Karamoko, who, bitten by fear, closed his eyes and swam toward the light, the light, the light.

When she rose I was perusing a novel by an author that I did not know.

"We promised that today would be easy," she said as she crossed the room toward me. She was barefoot and naked. Her nightgown, which was coiled up like a rope, was slung across her shoulders.

She stopped before she reached me and ponytailed her hair.

"African novels are too deep," she said as she wheeled the nightie like a sling. "They will strain a young boy's mind. Read some great American fluff."

"As if you have any."

"Send me some. And by the way you are allowed to kiss me

before I brush my teeth. In fact, kissing me as soon as I wake up is a basic cost of living here."

I kissed my thumb and dabbed her face. She laughed.

She opened one of the giant louvered windows, and for a moment she just stood there with her hands above her head, her palms against the frame, chin raised, hips thrown backward, catching light in her soft undulations, lost for a minute in thought.

As I laughed she bellowed: "Where is the light? Where is the light? Let's open them all and let in the light."

I watched her as she moved, the way in which her body parts delighted in their fleshiness, the softness of that ridge that women get below their navel, the overage on her counterweighted hips. All this I watched without moving.

She took a seat in the lounge, her dark thighs spreading on the saffron throw, playfully tossing and catching a java-printed pillow.

"Come," she said. "Sit with me."

I sat on the other couch, which was covered in a jade velour. Between us was a table. It was low and square and carved with radiating grooves.

"I have an idea," she said. "Let's forget yesterday. Let's forget last night. Let's forget the way we met. Let's forget everything and start over. Does it matter how we came to this? Or does it matter that we are here?"

"They matter in different ways."

There was a watering can filled with birds of paradise on the table. With knitted brows she sifted through the stems and stretched a perfect one to me.

"An offering of peace."

I touched it to my forehead to bless myself and felt a radiance within.

"I love you, Frances Carey."

"It is okay if you don't," she said while nodding slowly. "I'm a hard woman to love."

"But I do."

"You sounded like you need to make a point. Do you, really?"

"I didn't think I sounded any kind of way. Yes, I do."

"Why do you love me?" she asked.

With her dreads pulled back her dark lips seemed more pouty.

It was something I knew and believed but could not explain, like why rain falls or how planes fly or why hair grows faster if you cut it.

"Are we still forgetting everything?" I asked.

"Yes."

"It might sound pathetic," I said, aware that I was lying through a truth. "I love you for your house."

"Yes. Men always love women with their own place. I've noticed."

I felt bad when she said this, but I didn't show it because I knew she had been joking.

"Yes," I said while blowing her a kiss. "Houses say a lot about someone."

"Like what?"

"A house is a person's universe. It gives you an idea of what the world would be like if the owner were God. Your books say a lot. And your deck says a lot—the way you built it around the trees. And your flowers and your chairs and your paintings and your throws and your pillows all say a lot about a sense that this is a world that belongs to all peoples . . . and also that there are many kinds of beauty and beauty in many kinds of things." She began to beam. This was how she saw herself.

"And I don't feel bad for saying that I love you for your house," I added, "because I have loved other people for less compelling reasons."

"There were no others before me," she offered. "Before you either."

"Yes . . . yes . . . right . . . right."

"So tell me again about my house. For one thousand goodie points: What is it about my house?"

"It is the house that I would live in if I moved back to the island."

She rose and stretched her arms above her and released the lacy nightgown, shimmying as it splashed along her body, creaming her skin like a stream of milk. "Your answer is pathetic," she said with a smile, dressed and looking girlie now. "But I love you."

All morning I had been hearing someone moving on the floor below. Now the clink of pots and spoons approached.

"Miss Frances," came a timid voice from halfway down the stairs. "Mr. Carey ready for his breakfast, ma'am?"

"Are you, Mr. Carey?" Frances said, leaning back on the couch and raising her heels to the edge of the seat. The hem of her nightgown slipped over her knees, down to the middle of her thighs; there, it puddled like an awning filled with water, and I could see her glistening labia. She began to arc her back when I approached her; and sucked saliva through her teeth, and coughed and writhed a little when she felt my tongue inside her coily hairs, lifting them, pulling them, grazing like a bull.

Half an hour later when she heard her mistress scream, the helper raised her voice and said: "Miss Frances, there's a call."

From the sound of her arrival—she walked and breathed with heft—Claudette formed herself as a compact woman, middle-aged and thick-waisted.

But she showed herself to be dark and tall and curveless, a living exclamation point.

Her cotton shift was gray and stained with grease, but neatly pressed. There were buttons down the front and pockets large enough to hold thick mittens.

"Good morning, Mr. Carey—well, is afternoon by now. Good afternoon, Mr. Carey."

"Good afternoon, Claudette—"

Before I could ask she said, "Fine, thank you, sir." She spoke without lifting her head.

When she looked I was drawn into the sadness of her face, her pitted cheeks, her fragile chin, her eyes like open pods.

She gave the telephone to Frances, folded one hand inside the other and waited for the sign to be dismissed. It came when Frances turned away from her and said hello. At this point it struck me that I was undressed—which made me worry. What would become of this thing that had started so crazily and had gone on so crazily and was still going crazy after all the crazy things that had happened?

Could something this surreal have a real ending . . . an ending that would satisfy my need to prove that I had outgrown the patterns that had defined me all my life?

We both have complicated histories, I admitted. And if I were her and knew the things I knew about myself, I would not want me.

Then I was overtaken by another thought. I had always thought that if I should ever know about a woman all the things I knew about Frances, I would mark her as a fling and nothing more.

So why is it so different now? Why am I still here? Especially after she hit me? Is it for the thrill? Material for a play? My writer's need to find the narrative, the plot, in everything?

As Frances talked I went to the bed to soak up the aroma that had seeped out of her body and soaked into the sheets. I was not listening, but I heard.

Her latest venture was a line of skin care products. She was importing shea butter from Ghana. There was a problem with a shipment. The butter had come, but the supplier was insisting that the funds had been wired to the wrong account. In the last three days he had called her sixteen times from Accra.

"Fuck," she exclaimed when the call was over. "I hate doing business with my people."

"Never mind. It's okay. Come lie down with me."

She curled herself against me with her head beneath my chest, and I could feel her perspiration misting my skin as I stroked her flanks beneath the nightie.

She was heaving like a lioness whose encounter with a hunter had left her with some buckshot in her side.

"I will fix it for you," I promised. "Whatever it is. I will fix it. I will make it better for you."

Dressed now, she in a yellow *lappa* and floppy hat, me in a white T-shirt and latte-colored shorts, we went downstairs to eat.

The stairs were old. The steps were creaking and uneven. The balustrade had missing posts.

The lower floor, I saw, was not a place of whimsy. It was pervaded with a serious mood. Here the rooms were walled. The floors were made of stone. The ceiling was flat and low. The doors were either missing or ajar, and the paint was mapped with watermarks.

The windows were open, but the air was damp and cold. I stepped off the landing and followed Frances down a long and narrow corridor that seemed to halve the house.

To my surprise the kitchen was a modern room. Claudette was sitting on a chair between the double sinks and the center island, which was as long as an aircraft carrier and anchored by a Viking range.

"Claudette, what did you make for Mr. Carey?"

She opened a blue enamel pot and winced as if she saw an accident.

"Banku, ma'am."

"Didn't I leave a note that Mr. Carey was a vegetarian?"

Claudette looked at me and lowered her head, craning her neck like the faucet. I raised my brow and thought, Poor girl, this is unfortunate.

"I had forget, Miss Frances."

"Go and sit somewhere," Frances muttered. "Why do I ever let you do anything?"

"It's okay," I said, taking Frances by the elbow. "Never mind."

Now no one knew what to say.

"Claudette," I said to change the subject, "could I have a drink of water, please?"

She took a glass from the row of wooden shelving that stretched from wall to wall.

"It is not her fault," Frances said as she took her time to close the pot. "I should have done it myself."

"Never mind," I said when Claudette brought the water. "It's not a big deal."

Frances patted Claudette's shoulder.

"Sorry for speaking to you that way. That call was really upsetting. I took it out on you. Forgive me, please, my dear. But as you do that please make Mr. Carey an outside bath." She stroked my arm. "I will cook for him."

Claudette smiled weakly and left the room and soon returned with towels and what appeared to be a tool kit.

I followed Claudette out the door, up a flight of narrow steps and onto the concrete courtyard, a strip of bottle green between the royal blue of the house and the first of three retaining walls that carved the mountain into terraces.

I ducked beneath the laundry, which felt damp against my

skin, and followed Claudette from the courtyard up a flight of steps with landings on each level.

From there we took a garden path along a gradient fluffed with ferns and palms, arriving at a grove of almond trees that grew around a hollow, and there in a circle of whitewashed stones, on a platform made of concrete topped with Moorish tiles in white and blue, was a tub with flaring edges.

When Claudette moved toward an almond tree, I saw the plastic pipe that snaked along the ground from the direction of the house. It scaled the trunk and slid along a branch and ended in a dangling head.

The water was a steady silver stream. The droplets pinged the cream enamel. And as the water level rose the pings congealed into a sizzle.

I slung my clothes and towel on a multipointed iron hook suspended from a lower branch, as Claudette, in the manner of a trained domestic, found a reason to distract herself, looking only when she heard me slushing in the water, which had risen to my shins.

In the iron case—the tool kit—I found a wooden rack of salts and unctions sealed with cork in brown bottles labeled in fluttery script.

As Claudette walked away, her arms at her sides, her sandals dragging up the slope, I uncorked a bottle labeled GINGER MINT, poured some golden crystals in the bath and watched it quickly foam. Soon Claudette returned with a bottle of Australian shiraz.

With the aroma of the ginger and the tingle of the mint, and the bigness of the tub, and the warmth of the wine, and the chiming of the copper-colored almond leaves, I found myself believing I could fix it all for Frances. Fuck it, I would fix it all for Frances, then I'd fix it for myself.

I began to think without fear about my daydream, the one in

which I had sunk into the depths of the Atlantic and seen the ancestral bones and heard the chorus singing in a language from another life.

And I began to think of all the plays I had written and all the ones I wanted to write, and began to feel an integrated sense of power and possibility, a sense that I had made a little something of my life in defiance of my father's expectations.

"I didn't expect that I would have to cook for you," said Frances when she came to sit with me. "Not that I mind. I have taught Claudette so many things, but she always seems to forget. I will cook for you from now on, though. I promise."

We were facing each other in the tub. The added mass had brought the water level to my collar. Our legs slipped around and over themselves, sometimes showing just above the suds, which had grown warm in the sun.

"Cooking was a part of your promise," I replied. "You said that you would fuck your man and feed him and spoil him to death."

She closed her lids. Without the whiteness of her teeth and the brightness of her eyes her face disappeared into itself, and I was drawn again into the mystery of beauty, the *what* of it. In my head and before my eyes I saw her in different poses, in different moods, in different kinds of light. I decided that her *what* was her skin, not just the shade, but the temperature, the coolness of it. The blackness of her skin was almost frosty. Matte. So unreflective that it made you want to buy her jewelry to make her shine. Either that or make her smile to spark the lanterns in her eyes. Yes, the blackness was a part of it. There was the blackness and the brio of her high Egyptian nose.

She reached over the edge of the tub and poured some oil into the water.

"This stuff is really great," I said. "The packaging is wicked, too. Really nice and simple."

"Do you like it, really?" she replied. "This is a new thing I am doing. After lunch I'll take you to the office and you can see it all."

"So you make it here?"

"Everything."

"And you do it all yourself."

"A lot of these formulations have been around for thousands of years in some form or another. I mean, it is a part of what you grow up knowing your elders to do. I have always found it so amazing that all these do-good, save-the-planet companies can always find a way to use African people's knowledge to make a profit for themselves. But this money never comes our way. So I said, 'Why can't we cannibals make some cash?' "

"Are you in the stores?"

"No. I just started to bottle them three months ago. Before, I used to make them for myself. And people would always ask me what I use and so I started making things for people and they would bring their own containers. Completely organized and scientific."

"Do you have a name?"

"Well . . . not really . . . nothing sensible."

"And what about the names on the labels?"

"Those are just generics so I can find what I need to find when I need to find it quickly."

"Let me help you. I am big and strong. With good instruction I can lift a lot of boxes."

"Oh, I would love your help. Oh, that would be so cool. Do you know what. Let us make them characters. Let's give them names and funny histories. That would be such fun."

"Do you know Lu Chi's *Wen Fu*?"

"What is that?"

"It is an ancient Chinese text on writing. Lu Chi said a writer should 'collect from deep thoughts the proper names of things.' "

"That is brilliant."

She flicks her hand and splashes me with suds.

"There is a power in naming things."

"They say knowledge is power," she muses. "But even knowledge needs a name to know itself."

"Do you think you know yourself?" I asked.

"I do."

"So who are you?"

"I am a woman who has come to know herself through her mistakes." She opened her eyes and caught me off guard with the brightness of her smile. "And who are you?"

"A man who is still on the learning curve. There are so many men inside me, all of them crude constructions. I do not know myself. I never have. I have always been a stranger here. None of me has ever seemed to fit."

"Why is that?"

"I don't know. There are so many reasons."

"Share them with me. Unburden yourself. That is a part of spoiling you."

"I never felt as if my father loved me. A lot of it has to do with that. He didn't love me because he saw too much of himself in me. Although to me we have always been different."

"But what did he see in you?"

"We look alike."

"Was he smart?"

"Smart but fundamentally a brute."

"I did ask, didn't I? I am sorry. It was none of my business."

"It is, though."

She leaned her head and examined me.

"Is it?"

"It is. Because I love you."

"What is that to you? What do you mean when you love someone?"

I searched for her hands beneath the water, felt the eelish slickness of her thighs, then found a finger.

"I don't know what I mean," I replied. "I used to know, but I don't know anymore. Everything has changed now. The way I feel about you has changed everything. I used to say that love is like weather and not climate, that falling out of love is a natural thing. Now I am not sure that I believe that anymore. What I am saying is that I used to just know what love was just by a feeling. But I am getting the feeling now that love is like a spirit that takes you over, that it should feel almost like a religious conversion. The Bible talks about that, about testing the spirits that come to you, because not all of them are speaking the truth. Many spirits can come in the name of God. And what is God but love?"

She looked away and pursed her lips, smiled, then made a silly face.

"It depends on whose god you are talking about."

I gazed at the suds, the sky, the copper saucers of the almond leaves. My reply must not appear to be an insult or a challenge. "For me there's only one."

She shrugged, perhaps dismissively. "For me, I have to say that there are many."

I squeezed her hand and hoped to God I wouldn't let it go.

"I know," I said. "I know."

She swished around and placed her back against me.

"Is that a problem?"

She drew my arms around her.

"To tell you the truth," I said, "I don't really know. As I said, I don't know anymore about anything."

I was not lying.

"I don't care what you believe," she said.

"Why is that?"

"Let me put it this way. When my mother was born, the senior elder woman in her village looked at her and said, 'You are the returned child of your departed great-grandaunt.' Now, my mother grew up with that notion in her mind, that she was the returned child, the reincarnation of her great-grandaunt. Then when she was ten years old she went to Catholic school and she became more westernized, and one day she confronted this elder woman and said, 'I don't believe what you said about me being the returned child of my great-grandaunt.' And the elder woman said. 'That is all right. It is so whether you believe or not.' Now, at sixty-five my mother talks to her great-grandaunt all the time. Because now she has come to see that this is just a part of life. The elder woman never tried to evangelize my mother, even though she believed my mother was the returned child of a great ancestor. She did not care if my mother believed or not. Because for her it was a simple matter of stating a fact. In Christianity if you don't believe you go to hell. I was raised a Catholic. I know. The Western world is a world of dichotomy and contrast. Good versus evil. Black versus white. Secular and sacred. Holy and profane. Evangelism is a battle between good and evil. In the African world divides are not so strict. There the spirit world is not a world apart from the physical world. The spirits are not holy. They are just there. So to believe in spirits does not create any crisis in the way you see the world. There is no crisis. The spirit world just is. The spirits are here whether you like it or not."

"What about Islam?" I challenged.

"Islam is not an African religion. It came like Christianity, with murder and contempt for the African soul."

"So what do you believe?"

"Does it matter what I believe?" she asked. "Or does it matter that I love you without caring what *you* believe?"

"The two things matter very much to me."

"Carey," she said, lifting her feet out of the water and placing them on the edge of the tub, her toes waterlogged and pruny, "I do not have the most education in the world. I did not finish college. I am a simple woman who has tried to make sense of this world by trying out many things. There are people who might not take me seriously because they have seen me go through my phases." She was obviously referring to Kwabena. "They have seen me waste my time. They have seen me fuck up and fuck up badly. They have seen me break promises and heard me tell lies. But there are some things that I know. I know that I want to see a world in which Africa's sons and daughters respect our sacred bond. I want to see a world in which the Africans around the globe trade goods but also ideas." Her voice became strident. "We are being left behind by the rest of the world, Carey. They don't care about us. We have to start caring for ourselves. Nigeria has oil. Jamaica has bauxite. America has the scientists and money lenders. Why can't we own an aluminum plant? Why don't Jamaicans drink African beer? Why aren't black American legislators helping our governments to write the kind of constitution that made America great? Why aren't Howard and Hampton doing exchanges with the University of the West Indies and the University of Legon?"

"According to Fanon we are the wretched of the earth."

"We are not," she said. "We are not the wretched of the earth. We are simply the unbelievers. We do not believe in each other and we do not believe in ourselves. I know what I want, Carey, but I am not a politician. This land and this house that I have been taking my time to fix up is my own little queendom. I make the rules here. You don't have to believe in my way to be a part of my life, Carey. I cannot get the big boys with the big education to do their part, so I will begin with my own life. Carey, we should not let religion get between us. I am what I am and you are who you are, and the divine that lives inside us will answer to many names and will nourish itself on any sacrifice that we choose to bring, whether it's a wafer or some incense or the carcass of an animal."

"I hear you. I hear you."

She touched my chest. "But do you understand?"

Later, over lunch, she said again: "I don't care what you believe. I love you."

We were upstairs, on the deck, shaded by the trees. We were hungry and had opened a second bottle of wine and were eating with our fingers from a platter made of wood.

The bread showed hot grill marks on its golden crust, and we broke it and dipped it in the bowls of stew, and she told me the story of each dish. The red hot pepper was *kpape shito*. The spinach in the peanut sauce was *kontomreh*. *Akara* and *jollof* rice I knew.

"I know you don't care," I told her. "And I am grateful to you."

"It will work out, right?"

She held my arm and squeezed it.

"It will," I said.

"I know it will."

"It has to," I told her. "It must."

After lunch, we went to her office to talk about her salts and lotions. The journey, which was longer than I had expected, led us past the hollow where we had bathed, through an orange grove and over the lower ranges of the spur, which nosed down from the mountain face, cutting off the office from our view.

At first the going along the spur was gradual and we felt elated as we held hands and floated through the coolness of the bottle-colored shadow, which was broken here and there by shards of light.

At a point where a cotton tree lay sliced in two by lightning, the land began to swell and the path rose steeply, and we were happy when we came around a corner and approached the crest. There, at the top, the land descended smoothly into open ground, and we left the slope and trees behind and moved toward the house, holding hands and singing sixties reggae and seventies R&B.

The wind was coming smooth and low, and we felt it on our faces and in our hair, and we could hear the crabgrass crunching with each step.

From fifty yards away we saw the brilliant slatted whiteness of the chairs on the veranda, which was narrow and low with an overhanging roof supported by a row of slender columns.

It was a simple house, newish, with double rows of redwood louvers and a paneled door, not so much a house as a cottage.

We heard a yelp; and a khaki dog began to saunter up the driveway, which was made of pitch and was curbless.

"Hello, Puggy," Frances said. The dog began to bark. "That's Puggy," she said, pointing with our doubled fist. "He is one of my favorite dogs. He turned up one day and never really left. Do you have pets?"

"No."

"Why not?"

"I think I am holding out for children. They are like pets. Only thing is they grow up eventually and are able to feed and bathe themselves and go to the shop and bring you a juice from the fridge."

"So you don't have any kids yet?" she asked directly.

"Not that I know of."

I didn't like the way it sounded and I tried to correct myself.

"I don't have any children. But you can never know in this life."

"That's a difference between men and women, isn't it? Women always know where their children are."

She was right. And she could have made the conversation tedious. But she didn't. And I loved her even more.

The dog's excitement brought a man to the door. As Frances waved he made a visor with the edge of one hand and tucked his khaki shirt into his belted olive trousers.

Closer up I saw that he was old, with silver whiskers flecking copper skin and ears that drooped as if they had been weighted when he was a boy.

"Hi, Baboo," Frances shouted as we stepped into the shade. The old man took her outstretched hand in both of his and bowed before he turned to nod at me.

"Good eve-lin, Miss Frances," the old man said. His voice sounded like he'd coughed it from an itchy throat. "Good eve-lin to you, sah."

"Baboo is the watchman," she said. "He can't hear and he can't see, so I can trust him not to steal my things."

"I am the watchman," Baboo said, gloving my hand in his. "I fight in the war in the West India regiment. That time the white man didn't use to respect us and wanted us to only do supply. But our regiment almost mutiny and they put us on the line in Italy and France. We fight with the African. Y'ever hear about the African Rifle? We fight wid dem. Some good boys those were. They call there Kenya now. But we fight with them. Good soldiers them. Good people them. They come in just like we."

In my head Junior Reid was imploring, "One blood." We stepped off the veranda into the living room, which Frances used as her office.

"That's where I work," she said, pointing to a gray iron desk. We were sitting on an old brown couch. Beside us was a little fridge. Beside the fridge there was a row of metal cabinets heaped high with folders, books, and papers.

Pointing again she said, "And that's where my assistant sits when she decides to come to work."

The desks were right-angled. The assistant's desk formed the shorter side. Her piles of books and paper were set in stacks and

did not look like fallen leaves. There was no potted plant on top
of her computer.

"Is this where you spend most of your days?" I asked.

She leaned her head in my lap and I began to rub her bottom
through the *lappa*.

She opened her eyes but did not turn her head.

"Baboo gets really jealous," she warned. "You mustn't let
him see you do that."

"Are you serious?"

She closed her eyes again.

"He is convinced that I'm his wife."

"Is she dead?"

"That's the whole thing. She is alive."

"So how many people work for you?" I asked her as we
laughed.

"In total, maybe twenty. Most of them are out at sites though.
In the office, anywhere from three to six. It all depends."

"On what?"

"Sometimes I give people work to help them out. Of course, I
do the important things myself."

Baboo began to push the door. Frances straightened up. He
huffed and sucked his teeth, pretending not to see us.

"Trouble," she said, chuckling into her hand. "Didn't I tell
you? Come around the back. Let me show you where I make
my things."

Down the hallway we passed bedrooms used as storage space
for auto parts and tools.

In the washroom, across the passage from the kitchen, she
shoved aside some work boots stiffened by cement and led me
to the corner where the salts and lotions sat on racks in colored
plastic buckets by the sink.

In the kitchen three gray Formica tables set on slender folding legs were covered with brown bottles and sheets of labels.

We opened the back door and sat on the steps, drinking beer

and limeade out of Milo cans, brainstorming as we looked out on the croton hedge, feeling renewed . . . elated by love and the power of giving things their proper names.

When we left the sky was smoother than an iron's face. Perspiration wet my shirt. Heat pressed on my back. My scent rose up like steam.

Of all the names that we had chosen, our favorite was the Secret Oil of Atsede the Eritrean, who, we decided, was a negress with an oval face and feline eyes, and who, apart from being a servant of the Queen of Sheba, had tutored King Solomon in horsemanship and archery while earning favor as a gifted concubine.

"We should go swimming in the river," she said as we crossed the open ground toward the trees. Off to our right some goats were foraging in the knee-high grass.

"This reminds me so much of home," she said, opening her arms for emphasis.

"What about it?"

"The grass, the trees, the goats, the everything. Have you ever been to Africa?"

"Not yet. No. Well, yes and no. Does Morocco count?"

"You've been to Morocco?"

"No, I haven't. But I have been wanting to go for the longest time. I have friends from there."

I felt embarrassed.

"Why Morocco?" she asked. "Why not somewhere else?"

"Why not Morocco?" I said too quickly.

"I'm not trying to be difficult, darling." She sprinted a bit ahead of me and talked while walking backward. "I haven't forgotten that we made a promise to be nice. I am not trying be tedious or anything."

"I don't think you're being tedious," I replied, shaking my

head quickly. I loosened the last of the buttons and my shirt flapped open. The perspiration felt like crawling crickets. "Sometimes questions make you look inside yourself and think about yourself a little more. And sometimes you don't like what you see. Why did you ask?"

She reached out and wiped my face with her palm and rubbed the sweat in her hair. I took her hand and spun her around, hooked my arm in hers.

"I asked because I was sure that you had gone," she said.

"Well, I am sorry to disappoint you."

"No, it's nothing like disappointment, baby. I'm just getting to know you."

"And what does going to Africa have to do with anything. There are many other things that could have come before that, like 'Are you seeing anyone?' Or 'Have you ever hit a woman?' Or 'Is it okay for you to keep pets in the house?' "

"You are getting annoyed."

"No, I am not getting annoyed."

"Yes, you are."

"Okay, I am."

"I guess I'll just be quiet then."

"No . . . don't do anything like that."

"I don't want to annoy you, though."

"I am not annoyed."

"But you just said you were."

"Okay . . . I am."

"Which is what I said."

I understood my state of mind. The truth is that I wished that I did not. When I had named the concoction the Secret Oil of Atsede the Eritrean I had spoken in great detail about the history of Ethiopia, most of it gleaned from books like the *Kebra Negast*, the oral history of the Ethiopian kings.

But all along there had been something in her question that had made me seem invalid.

Why had I not been to Africa? Because I was afraid—afraid that I would come away unrecognized, unmasked, and unwanted.

Farther on along the path, at a point where we could see the almond grove around the tub, Frances said, "I was asking about Africa because I think I will be going soon and I want you to come."

Defensive now, I challenged.

"Why are you going?"

"I am going to speak to my shea butter man. I need to straighten this whole thing out. He is very powerful. He is not the kind of man you want to cross."

"How do you mean powerful?"

"He's a big man."

"He threatened you?"

"Not directly. But some things are just not good. A man of his power can reach very far."

Later, upstairs, as we faced each other on the couches in the lounge she added, "This man has the kind of power that you do not understand. He is what we call a *futah*."

Her face was partly hidden by the vase of birds of paradise. I placed it on the ground, leaving on the table a pile of books and magazines, an ashtray with a burned-out spliff, a backgammon board, a plastic pitcher, and glasses with iced water.

Six of the ceiling fans were going, their rotors raging like a fleet of helicopters.

I placed my elbows on my knees.

She flopped her hands in her lap, began to speak, stopped, turned her head outside and gazed through the open louvered windows to the deck. She leaned backward in the chair, pulling the throw with her weight.

"It is not the kind of power that I think we should discuss," she said. "I'm afraid you will think I am being stupid or something. Maybe you will get nervous. I don't want to end up feeling awkward again. I don't want to go back to that vibe again. Can we not talk about it? Please?"

"Try me."

"I am not ready to talk yet."

"Go ahead."

I was trying to maintain myself. At times I felt controlled. Then suddenly there would be panic, like the stomach of a man who had eaten meat declared unclean by his religion.

"Talk to me, Frances. I want to know."

"You are not ready to hear this, Carey."

"Yes, I am."

"I don't think so."

"I am the best expert on me."

"Okay," she said. "What do you want to know?"

"Are you talking about obeah—"

"Go ahead," she said. "Be condescending. Be simple-minded. Be crude."

I responded through the flurry.

"I didn't mean to—"

"It's not you," she said, wiping her face with her hand. She shook her head and sucked her teeth. "It's me. It's my thing. You don't have to get involved."

"But I am involved."

"And why is that?"

"By being involved with you."

"I appreciate you for saying that."

I felt insulted now.

"What do you mean?"

"I don't know what I mean," she said, looking down at her hands. She looked up again.

"I know what you mean," I told her. "I know exactly what you mean. You mean that somehow I am not African enough to understand; that somehow I am not spiritual enough to get it;

that this kind of thing is bigger than me. Well, it is not, because I have something called common sense."

"Don't be mean to me right now," she said. "I need you to be nice to me right now. This thing is very scary."

I reached for the glass. As I held it to my face her image was multiplied and distorted through the beads of water, a fly's-eye view of life.

"What do you want me to do?" I asked.

"Make me feel protected."

"What will that take?"

"I don't know."

"Okay . . ."

She gloved her head in her hands and began to speak through the cracks in her fingers, leaning forward now, her shoulders round.

"I don't know why I am feeling so weak and weepy. This is really not my style."

I sat beside her and drew her close, guiding her head to the scoop of my collar as I rubbed her leg, my hand moving like an eraser, a distraction really, the kind of thing one does to keep a child from noticing the angle of her broken thumb.

"It is okay to feel weepy," I told her. "I will make you feel better."

"It's okay," she said eventually. "I can sit by myself. I live alone. I have been alone. I can take care of myself."

I sat across from her again.

"What do you want me to do?" I said. "Whatever it is, I will do it. How much do you owe him for the shipment? I will take care of it."

"It's not about the money, Carey."

"Okay, then. I am sorry."

She threw her arms in the air and began to walk away, and I reached across and held her arm. "Stay."

She sat down again, sucking on her bottom lip, gathering and folding her hem.

"What do you want me to do?" I said. "Come on, baby, use your words. Tell me what you want."

She looked up and smiled shyly, blinked, held my stare and blinked again, and began to cry in silence, shaking her head as one would in disbelief.

As I thought of what to do she grabbed the book I had been reading and said, "I don't want to go through another night like last night. Me and you in bed like brother and sister. Me reaching for you and you pushing me away. I just want to lose myself in you tonight. I just want to start everything over. I just want to feel like a virgin again."

She opened the book and pointed to a passage.

"That is what I want. If you do me like that I will be fine."

The beast erupted from the undergrowth and leaped. Its jaws were wide open. Its claws held up high. He charged toward it with his spear pressed hard against his pounding chest. With its mighty claws the beast smote his spear away and he fell upon the beast with rage. The gods were moved by this bravery and they changed a leaf into a dagger and he sunk it in the beast; but the taste of its blood was like new palm wine. It was too precious to spill. So he withdrew the magic weapon and pledged to protect the beast with his life.

"I will do you like that," I said, taking a sip of the water again. My throat was so tight that the water just pooled in the back of my mouth, and as we sat there, staring through each other into the eye of our interior lives, Claudette brought the telephone.

I went out on the deck and found myself against my will considering something Kwabena had said: *Oh, that is completely bogus, Carey. Frances doesn't take it seriously. Lemme just explain something to you before you go and fuck your life. If there is one thing I know about Frances it is this. She will do and say anything to get a man to fuck her. That is how she was. That is how she is. That is how she will always be.*

Could this be what this is all about?

But what if I was wrong? What if this woman, on this day, with her own rationale, had decided that this was in fact what would make her feel better? And what is so wrong with a woman wanting love as a distraction? Hadn't that been the pattern of my life?

The truth is that my relationships have always been experimental. Not experimental in the way of kinky. Experimental in the sense that I seduced not so much to enjoy but to prove, to prove that women wanted sex as much as I, that women were as desperate to get it . . . would hide in the linen closet at the dinner party, would take it on a side street on the hood of a car, would come downstairs and brace against a wall while their husbands and children watched TV.

And this is not to say that these relationships had been about just sex. There had been trips together and dinners out and cards for no reason and Sunday morning searches for the perfect portobello mushroom.

But these relationships had been experimental—because I had always kept the distance of observer.

Sarah once told me that I made her feel like an object. What she didn't realize was that she was a subject.

I would try different ways of hurting her—then find the most efficient way to sweet her up. A scarf? A silly toy? A meal? A sonnet quickly drafted on good paper? And this is how I came to know the depths of her, how I came to know her better than she knew herself.

I was engrossed but disconnected, focused from a distance. Attentive but just passing through. The painter of a portrait.

Thus leaving, for me, has always been easy. I have walked away from many things and many people. The world is filled with subjects for a fascinated eye.

In this way I am my father. He would pull you here and poke you there to feel the joints where you would break. Then he would find the thing that glued you, that would bind you while you healed.

But you never really healed, did you? You are still wounded. You are still hurt. There are many broken places in you. Many lacerated parts. He filled your lungs with toxic words. Now you are so sick inside. There is something swelling up inside you. Eating you up. Soon you will be nothing.

That night I lay in bed and waited for Frances to come. She slipped into her space beside me, clothed in nothing but a waist bead and some ankle bracelets made of bells.

She lay on her stomach and handed me a jar of oil.

"I want to leave blood on the sheets," she whispered.

"It will hurt," I replied.

"I know it will."

Her muscles were taut. The bells began to chime.

"It will hurt a lot."

"I know. I know. Just talk me through it. Play with my clit to distract me. But not too much pain, okay. Not too much pain."

"There will be some."

She ground her face into the pillow.

"I know. I know."

"But you want it."

"Yes. You wouldn't understand how much. I've given too much of myself to undeserving people. In my queendom you are my king, Carey. The king must eat of special portions. No one must eat of his supper. No one has had this supper, baby.

No one. Only you. Do you want it? Do you want it?" She reached between my legs. "Yes, you want it. God, you are so big. There will be so much pain."

"I will take my time. I promise . . . I will take my time."

"Take your time, please."

"I will."

"I have heard that when it's in you can be a little rough. That you can play at being angry with me. You can slap me and pull my hair and ask me whose I am." She reached between my legs again. "And I will tell you I am yours. I have come to you as a sacrifice."

The doors to the deck were open. The sound of the river was steady. The wind was soughing through the trees. The leaves filled the room with pulsing shadows.

My lubricated finger made her shudder. In the morning there was blood and scattered shells and broken beads.

The sound of her singing drew me out of bed the next morning; and I went out on the deck and looked over the railing and saw her sitting cross-legged on a boulder, her dreads French-braided down her back. She was playing a guitar, and I felt a twinge as I remembered when I had first seen her.

She had saved my life, had kept me going until now. Until this. This thing of value, as imperfect as it was.

Dawn had barely lifted. The air was cool. Dew tinged the greenest leaf with silver. The low light was bringing out the beauty of life, from the contours of the hills to the genius encoded in the pattern of the spider's web.

She stood on the rock, slung the guitar on an overhanging branch, rolled up her gray sweatpants to her knees and waded in the water. A bamboo rod was wedged between two stones.

"I didn't know there were fish in the river," I shouted.

"Perch and mullet," she replied. "Do you eat fish?"

"Sometimes."

"So I thought. I will make you some for lunch. Come," she said. "Come. Come and fish with me."

And in a flash of clarity I knew my love for her had changed. Before it was a bracelet, a roomy set of interlocking loops, beautiful with many points of weakness. Now my love was like the ring of flesh that she had given me—continuous, snug, and unbroken.

"I love you," I said. "I love you."

"I know," she said, "I know."

"It's a very great thing when you know."

"There is nothing more beautiful than that."

"So who is the sweetest girlfriend in the world?"

"Who?" she asked with a smile.

"No one else but you."

"So come," she said. "Come now."

I glanced over my shoulder.

"I don't know how to get down there."

"Go downstairs," she said, "and follow your nose."

I did as I was told and made my way downstairs. The house was silent. Claudette was not there. And the only sounds were the creaking of the stairs and the shooshing of the river and the beating of my heart in my ears.

She had told me to follow my nose. But when I stepped off the stairs onto the landing I did not know where to go. I went to the kitchen. I could not find the key for the door. I took the passage to the stairs again, amused now that the house was such a puzzle.

I began to feel a deep attachment to the place. There was so much here to build and discover. I began to wander through the rooms and passages, projecting how different they would look with my things.

Where would my plants go? Where would my books go?

Which pieces of art would go on which walls? Which room would be my study? Which room would be my gym? And the baby's room? There had to be a room for our child. Upstairs, of course. Upstairs. With mum and dad.

The thought of the baby was light at first and then it became quite heavy. I leaned against a wall and thought about the meaning of a child, and asked myself if it would be fair to the child for me to go ahead with this love with this woman that I knew in a way that would not make sense to my closest friend, a woman I had known for three days, a woman I had known perhaps in a previous life.

And as I thought of this I thought of all the children I had lost, the little blobs of blood miscarried, the knots of muscle that were rousted from their mothers at the clinic, the half-white boy who came to term but was lynched by his mother's umbilical cord.

I felt myself sliding to the floor, found myself on my knees, heard myself asking God's forgiveness . . . God the white man in the sky.

As I prayed I felt my nostrils burning. At first I thought it was the tears. But as I walked through the house again, the smell remained.

As I came along the passageway the scent became a little stronger, and as I turned my head to see if I could see the smoke I noticed, for the first time, a door beneath the stairwell.

Curious, I opened it, and saw to my unease and great disorientation that Frances kept an altar to her gods.

The floor was sprinkled with cornmeal. A circle had been drawn with a finger or a stick. Around this circle was another one defined by bowls of water, mounds of peas, flasks of rum, black candles in white saucers, oleander petals, and bundles of cloth.

Beyond this was another circle made of chicken carcasses. And in the center of it all there was a stool trimmed in dyed raffia. The seat was prickled with hammered nails on which was placed the severed head of a goat, a big white ram with eight-inch horns and candles set deep in its wide eye sockets.

"We have to talk," I said when I found my way to the river.

She was standing on the shallows with a basket full of fish.

I told her that I could not be with her unless she underwent baptism. She told me no. I asked her why. She asked me why she should when I did not believe in my God myself. I told her that I did, which made her laugh, which made me shout, which made her laugh some more, which made me tell her all the things Kwabena told me, which made her cry, which made me sneer, which made her shake her head in disbelief, which made me stop and think, which made her curse at me, which made me leave her house.

I left everything except the clothes in which I dressed myself. I did not want to touch anything that had been in her house.

I went to New York and then I went to see my mother.

CHAPTER TWENTY-THREE

Six weeks have passed. And although I feel quite welcome here, I know it is time to leave. Simply, I am depressed and my mood is quite contagious.

I have not been to the hill since July. Now it is late August. I have not been eating with the family. I have not been having many meals at all. The little that I take is hard to keep down. I have lost the will to run or to coach the children. All I want to do is write.

I bought a laptop. With my mobile phone I use it to buy the things I need.

At night I write love poems in a composition book. The ink is royal blue, but there is something pink about the verse, a bubblegum disposability that in the past would have embarrassed me.

These are awful poems full of artificial color. Read aloud, I am sure they would rot my teeth.

In the last three weeks Kwabena has been staying down in Greelyville till way into the night. We hardly see each other. We no longer have the urge to talk.

It cannot be easy for him. What are his choices? How can he

tell me to forget her, when clearly he has not? And what does this mean for his marriage? If Nazia found out what would she think?

She was watching the tape with Kwabena when I lurched against their door. Why was Kwabena watching Frances? Does he watch her all the time? Should I try to find the tape and look at her myself?

One afternoon, after weeks of barely speaking to me, Nazia comes to the door.

"We have been missing each other," she says. "I thought it would be good to come." Beneath the bill of her denim cap, her eyes are soft in dark brown circles. It wouldn't be right to shut her out, no matter how politely.

I step away to let her in. She does not move.

"Apologize to the kids for me. I really didn't mean to—"

"You don't have to explain anything. I just thought you might want to talk to somebody. Kwabena hasn't been around." She looks away then looks at me again. "I hope I am not intruding. I am getting a sense that you are not all right. That . . . that there is something that you need to say."

She takes off the cap and shoos a strand of hair along her temple.

"Is it hot?" I ask.

She glances around me. "The windows aren't open," she replies. "And it is noon in the middle of August. It is ninety-four degrees outside. It is very hot."

"Are you okay?"

"Yes . . . yes . . . I am."

She steps to the side and peers inside the room, at the furniture she and Kwabena bought together piece by piece.

"What are those?" she asks while pointing. The dining table is stacked with composition books. The tubular chairs are stacked with novels that I have ordered off the internet and have not had the chance to read.

"I have been writing by hand."

"What are you writing?" she asks.

"Poems."

"About love?"

"Why do you think so?"

I close my eyes and bow my head and hear her coming, the creaking floor, the padding feet. Then there is the coolness of her shadow and the smell of her skin. And I open my eyes and see her toes in front of mine, the segments long and slender, the joints full and slightly wrinkled, with little tufts of hair.

"Why do you think that I am in love?"

Has Kwabena told her?

"I did not say you were in love," she says. "But ... are you?"

"Yes. I am."

She looks me up and down.

"Does she know?"

"She does and she doesn't."

"Tell her then," she urges. "Be bold. That is my new mantra. I have been quiet for too long. It doesn't make you happy."

I ignore the unsubtle invitation to discuss her life. Discussing her life would mean discussing Kwabena. And discussing Kwabena would confuse me. Lately I have begun to imagine him as my rival, sometimes as my antagonist, begun to analyze and question our friendship, the *how* of it, the *why* of it, avoiding the question of *therefore*.

"This love is not an easy love," I lament. I smile as an afterthought to satisfy her need to see me looking better.

"There are complications?" she presses.

"Many. Too many."

She shakes her head and attempts to say something that does not want to come out. Eventually she settles on something that, from her expression, she believes is deep and charged with meaning.

"Love is fairly easy," she says. "It is the choices that are hard."

"I have a lot of them to make," I mumble.

"Perhaps she does as well."

"I don't know."

"If she is in love as well she must."

She lifts my face, balancing my head with stiff but gentle fingers.

"Look at me," she whispers. I feel a spurt of breath against my nose. "I have seen you worse. Remember that. Always."

The reference is clear. She was the one who revived me when I tried to kill myself.

"I was very frightened," she whispers.

Neither of us can hold it so we look away.

"But that was a long time ago." She pats my cheek and leaves. At the door, she holds the handle, her body kept in profile, her face fixed in my direction. "The children want to see a movie later. Would you like to come?"

"Thanks, but no. I have to write."

"I will check on you before I leave."

"Bye-bye."

When she comes I pretend to be asleep.

Her knocks grow loud then fade into the dots of an ellipsis. In khakis and a tank top, I am seated at the dining table writing awful poems.

The windows are open. If she walks around the house she will see me. I walk on tiptoe to the bed, test each step before committing, feeling quite embarrassed. I am the one who overstayed. Yet she is the one to feel unwanted.

"Carey . . . Carey . . . Carey are you there?"

"Yes," I say from the bottom of my throat. I turn my face toward the wall to add some muffle.

"It is Nazia. Are you coming?"

Her voice is reasoned but insistent.

"What time is it?"

"Eight o'clock. The movie starts in half an hour."

"That's late for the children."

"It's summer. It's okay. Are you coming?"

"What are you guys going to see?"

"It's for the children. Does it matter?"

"Where is Kwabena?"

"In Greelyville, I guess. I don't know. He's already disappointed us. Clearly you are going to do the same."

I am guilted out of bed. I open the door.

"What do you mean?"

She begins to smile, then changes her mind. She wipes her hand across her settling face.

Soon it will be dark.

"He called to say he would be back from Greelyville soon. That was at three. He gets so involved with these projects. There has to be time for us. Can you tell him that? As a friend? That he has to spend more time with us?"

"If you want me to, I'll tell him."

"I hope he listens to you. He doesn't listen to me."

"Enjoy the show. Tell the kids—"

"I'm sorry."

She begins to shake her head and mutter in a language that I do not understand, perhaps her native Urdu or Swahili. She paces back and forth. She is wearing boots and jeans tonight. Anxious, she smacks her hip, hurts herself, and blows her palm to cool it.

"It's not you," she says.

I fold my arms. I have never seen her act this way.

"It's me. It's my problem and I am making it yours."

"Okay, tell me, Nazia. What is going on?"

"Kwabena is having an affair."

She has never lied to me. Neither has Kwabena—until now. The play was cancelled weeks ago she has discovered and he is staying even later down in Greeleyville?

"It could be something else," I lied.

"Like what?"

CHAPTER TWENTY-FOUR

"Ask me something serious," Kwabena dares.

We are standing on the hill behind the house in late afternoon on the following day. It is humid and hot. The sky looks scrubbed. Traffic is thick on the streets below.

"I am not accusing you of anything, Kwabena. I am not trying to come between you and your wife. If you are sleeping with somebody it is not my concern. I just want you to know that she knows. You need to cover your ass or cut that woman off."

"I'm sure that Nazia would like to do the cutting." He holds his chest and laughs. "You can't be serious, Carey. Me? Kwabena? An affair? With whom?"

There is a smugness here that strikes me as performance.

I noticed it this morning over breakfast. As I entered the kitchen from off the porch he bellowed: "Lazarus has risen from the dead."

Kwabena has always been ironic. Ironic but never smug. One is witty. One is mean. The difference between flirtation and harassment.

"So where would she get this idea?" I insist. I ease up off the tree and move toward him, past him, circle him, forcing him to turn around and face me once again.

"I should ask you. You seem to know her more these days. She flew to you under cover of night."

"I'm trying to help you. Nothing more. If you don't want my help then say that. But don't tell me rubbish like that. Don't put my loyalty on trial. When you do that you make it seem as if you're trying to change the subject. That is the kind of thing that guilty people do."

He begins to fold his sleeve above his elbow, muttering to himself. The shirt is powder blue. I have no sleeve with which to fidget. There is nothing of authority in a tank top.

"I understand what you are trying to do," he says. "I understand what you are trying to do. You are trying to somehow pick a fight with me. You are somehow trying to end our relationship by forcing me to be cruel. Because whether you like it or not that is really what you are doing."

"You have it completely wrong."

"But that is the only thing I can think of. Because I cannot understand your choices. First, you discuss me with my wife behind my back. Second, you approach me in this stealthy way. There is this attitude that is disgusting me. This sense that what you are doing is trying to catch me in a lie. That you are trying to manipulate me. And I don't like that. I have seen you do it with women. It is something that you do ... manipulation. Don't act as if you're trying to catch me, Carey. Say what you have to say. What did she tell you?"

"That I can't reveal. All I'm trying to do is save you from an ambush. I just want you to be prepared."

"There you go again, Carey," he says, stroking his goatee. "You are accusing me."

"I am not accusing you."

He looks at me, looks away, shakes his head, looks at me again, wipes his mouth, smiles, and answers, "And how is this related to Frances?"

"It is completely unrelated to Frances."

"Of course it is related to Frances."

"Okay. How is it related to Frances?"

"Apparently everything is related to Frances. The world revolves around Frances."

"You are making this a personal thing."

"How could it be less than personal? You are making a personal accusation against me. You are insisting that I am lying when I am telling you the truth. There is no other way to take it but personally."

"You haven't been spending time with your wife and children, Kwabena. Where the fuck have you been?"

"What gives you the authority to speak for my wife?"

"What?"

"Don't try to overstep certain boundaries, Carey. It could get you into trouble. Friend or no friend. Nazia is my wife."

"Then treat her that way."

"Carey, if you were really concerned about my wife and children you wouldn't be—"

He spits at the root of the tree, and with his shoes begins to cover it with leaves.

"Wouldn't be what, Kwabena? What are you talking about?"

"You know exactly what I am talking about." He drops his arms and takes a step and folds his arms again. "Carey, you have been putting us through hell. We cannot sleep at night. Do you know what Nazia said to me a week ago? She said that she was nervous. I asked her what about. She said that she was worried about you being out there without anyone. And when she said this at first I didn't know what she meant. But when I put on my glasses and looked at her face I knew exactly what she was saying. The *anyone* that she was talking about was a psychiatrist. Do you know what she told me?" He points in my direction. "Do you know?"

I swallow hard.

"Say what you have to say, Kwabena."

He shoves his hands in his pockets and begins to circle me, forcing me to turn. Now the city is behind me.

"Do you really want to hear?" he challenges. "She said I should ask you to leave because she was worried that being alone in the cottage by yourself, considering what she called *your history*, might make you liable—"

He stops himself.

"She didn't say 'liable,' " he begins again. "She said 'inclined' . . . inclined to get depressed. Then she ran scenarios of all that could happen. Worst case, of course. And I should have followed my mind and stopped her. But I didn't. Do you know what she said?"

"How the fuck would I know?"

"She said that she was worried that you might lose it and cause some kind of harm . . . harm us or harm yourself or harm the kids. She asked me to ask you to go, Carey. And I couldn't face up to it, man. That is why I have been avoiding you. I haven't been doing the rehearsal in Greelyville for weeks now. But that has been my excuse. I have been lying to my wife on your behalf, my brother. They said one of the actors was caught with drugs. I don't believe the story. I think they trumped it up because they thought the guys were having too much fun." He opens his palms and shrugs again. "Is that what this is about? She has found out that the play is off and that I am still going down to Greelyville? Is that it? Tell me. Is that it? Because if that's it then we no longer have a problem."

I want to speak but I cannot. I feel as if the muscles in my chest have turned to bone. I am hurt. I am winded. But most of all I am suspicious.

If before I wanted Kwabena to be innocent, I want him to be

guilty now. I want revenge. I want revenge because he lied to me about Frances. She was not abused.

"Kwabena," I bluff, "she knows the woman's name."

He fans me off.

"Stop playing."

He has to work at being mean. For me it comes with ease. I will break him down. He should not fuck with me.

A gust of wind begins to shake the trees.

"I am not sure if she has both names," I continue. "But one should be enough. I have been in this kind of shit before. It is not about whether or not she can use the name to find the person. It is whether or not you are calm the first time she mentions that name. A bad reaction can fuck you, can take you right down."

Maps of sweat begin to trace themselves along his shirt.

"Carey—"

"Kwabena. Shut up and listen."

"I don't know."

"That's why you need to listen."

"Okay."

"First of all, have you ever called her from the house?"

"Look," he says, giggling, "I don't know where this is going. Neither you nor Nazia can make me have an affair, Carey. I am not having an affair. It is that simple." He begins to flex his brows. "But whenever I am ready to take that step I will come and talk to you."

"I am trying to help you save your marriage, man. If you called her from the house then there's a record."

"You are not ready to listen, Carey. You just want to talk. So you are just saying whatever comes to mind."

"I wish that were the truth, Kwabena. You are in fucking trouble."

"You think?"

"I know."

"What do you know, exactly?"

He studies my face, the maps of sweat congealing now, joining his sleeve with his pocket, his pocket with his yoke.

"I can help you," I say. "But I need you to be honest."

"Honest," he replies. "How ironic."

CHAPTER TWENTY-FIVE

Burdened by the weight of revelation, I slump down on the sofa bed and think about the things I need to do. It is clear. I have to go.

By the tulip-shaded lamp beside the sofa bed, I take stock of what I need to pack.

Having arrived with almost nothing I have acquired many things, almost all of which are scattered on the floor: shoes, clothes, books, a mini CD player, a water filter, an electric guitar, a portable amp, a weight bench, a blender, a juicer, a coffee machine, six hundred pounds of weights—and nothing in which to pack them but the olive canvas knapsack on the lacquer coffee table.

There is so much to do. I won't be able to leave here for days. But can I really stay here tonight, knowing that she thinks that I am crazy, that I am a threat? That I would hurt her children.

I lean over and remove my boots. With my nose against my underarm I note that I must shower.

When Nazia came to ask me to the movies she did not come inside. She remained outside the door. What was stopping her from coming in? The boots fall loudly on the floor. And what was her earlier visit about?

With my feet up on the table now I think about the time we talked about the poems. She was curious about my inspiration. Does she know more than I think she knows? Does she know about me and Frances? Does she know about Frances and Kwabena? Has she made all these links? Playing the fool to catch the wise?

Of the night I tried to kill myself her words were: *I was very frightened.*

She was frightened then, and she is frightened now. She thinks that I am a maniac.

But this is not what saddens me. I am saddened because I have always known her to be open. The way she forced Kwabena into asking me to leave was hypocritical. Why him? Why not her? I am the friend of both of them.

Now I am angrier at her than at Kwabena. If she hadn't told me that she thought Kwabena had a mistress I would not have known. I would have gone off to New York with a single burden—Frances Carey. Now because of Nazia I have two.

The fact of the matter is that Nazia, based on what she knows, should not have shared her thoughts with me. She did not have the evidence to spoil a man's good name.

As it turns out, Kwabena is involved. But that was my discovery. The truth is that his mistress does not live in Greelyville. And he does not see her during the time that he is supposed to be rehearsing. Furthermore this woman isn't new.

She lives in their old subdivision, and has been his mistress for years.

It begins to rain. At first the water makes the sound of dull collisions. There is lightning; then the water starts to hiss.

The rain evokes the recollection of the night before I left to ride with Frances back to Kingston, after fucking for the very first time. And I say fuck without apology. It is the word that she should use.

Fuck. Yes. *Fuck* is a sexy word. Sexier when you're not

fucking. Sexiest when it invites the fuck, like: "Babe, I just want you to fuck me."

The word *fuck* is really sexy when you're sitting in a room with your feet up on a table, and the room is kind of dark, and the single light is bringing out the texture of the brick, and the window is ajar, and the wind is lashing like a tongue.

Do you know what you do when that happens? You lick your palm. You watch it glistening in the light. You slip your hand inside your fly.

When you realize that your woman's flesh is wetter than your palm you lick your palm again. Then you touch yourself again and you wet your palm again. And you squeeze your cheeks together and you arch up off the chair, offering up yourself the way she lifts her body to your lips like buttered bread.

You hook your thumbs in your waistband. Tug your jeans off your waist. You watch your muscles tensing through your skin. You spit into your palms and rub yourself along your belly. You rub your chest. You rub your thighs. You keep your equilibrium. All the pressure on your neck. You breathe in spurts.

You soap your cock with raw saliva, coaxing veins to show themselves.

Do you know what you think of when you do this in a room awash with shadow on a muggy rainy night?

You think of all the things you like, the little things that turn you on . . . stretch marks . . . tan lines . . . a pouch below the navel . . . birthing scars . . . beauty spots . . . any kind of sex that leaves you bruised or scarred or crying.

Then you start to think of certain people doing certain things. The women who you've fucked already surface in your head, some of them without their names, others with no sense of time. Then the memories of the sweetest one come through.

Now your palm begins to tighten round your cock. You make a proper fist. You are a soldier with a dagger. As you stab yourself you smell your woman's blood. She lives in you. You are thrusting in her softest parts. You put it in. You sink it down. You twist it. Searching. Searching. Searching for the pelvic bone. But there is no bone. Just softness. Only softness. Only flesh and fat and water.

"Carey. Carey. Carey, are you there?"

Jesus Christ. It's Nazia.

I remove the sweating tank and wipe myself. I get a clean but rumpled shirt. There is no time to do the buttons. She is shouting. It is raining. She is wet.

There is a weight between my legs. There is a bulge.

"Carey! Carey!"

"Hold on. I'm coming."

I flip my cock and trap the head inside the waistband of my jeans.

She kicks and shoves the door, and I discover it was open.

In the dimness of the room she is a shadow trembling with her hands atop her head, the shape of her body obscured by a mannish mackintosh with reflective taping on the hem and sleeves.

Can she tell what I was doing?

"Fuck you, Carey. Fuck you."

Jesus Christ. She knows. Kwabena has betrayed me.

"I have to fucking talk to you." She slaps her hands against her thighs. "This fucking thing . . . this fucking marriage . . . this fucking you."

I have never heard her curse before.

"Nazia, close the door and calm yourself." I am sounding too cool, too much like the guilty informer. "Nazia, what the hell is wrong with you?"

She moves toward me with her hands still by her side. Her face is set. Her eyes are hard. She passes close without touching me and stands beside the window.

With the light on her I see the center stitching on the raincoat and the fuchsia brightness of the sari that is plastered to her legs. She is standing in a puddle. The rain is blowing in.

I button my shirt and fold the sleeves.

"Okay, what's the matter?"

"Don't fucking speak to me."

She does not look or move.

"Can I help in any way?"

"You can help by leaving. Just leave as soon as you can. Leave tonight. Tomorrow is too far away. Just get out of my fucking house. Just get out of my fucking life."

I begin to play at packing while I watch her, gathering up things and placing them in some kind of order, shirts with pants, books with music. But there is nothing in which to pack them. Now I need to ask her for her help, and I cannot face her anymore.

"Carey, did I give you any messages?"

I am partly kneeling on the bed. My eyes are pulled along the bricks toward the profile of her face. Her hair is wet and clinging. Water streams along her face.

Lightning flashes and she blinks. Her skin pleats at the corner of her eye. Her top lip rises to her arcing nose. One foot is forward. She has her elbows on the sill, her chin supported by a doubled fist.

In the presence of my bulge her beauty is embarrassing.

"What you did was wrong," she says. She slowly turns toward me. Rainwater slaps her face. This pains me. "I didn't ask you to speak to Kwabena."

"You did."

"Stupid me. I thought you would use discretion. I asked you to ask him to spend time with us, and now you have wrecked my marriage. I have never seen him this way before. He stormed into the house and shoved me, Carey. What the fuck did you tell him?"

I leave the bed and walk toward her. I lean against the wall. She cannot see the bulge. We are close enough to touch.

"I told him you think he is having an affair."

"Is that what I asked you to do?"

"No. You didn't."

"Why did you do it?"

"I really don't know."

"Well, it doesn't matter now because the shit has hit the fan."

"Cursing doesn't suit you."

She undoes the coat.

"You don't know me, really, Carey. I curse all the fucking time. I just don't do it around my children or my husband. I curse when I am alone, when this fucking mess that is my life is mine alone to figure out. I need a cigarette."

"You smoke?"

"When I can."

"I don't have any myself."

"Don't fuck with me. I smelled the smoke when I was here the other day. When did you start smoking again?"

"The other day."

"I thought all you smoked was marijuana?"

I get the cigarettes from a dirty shirt. I linger, inviting her to sit. She draws me back toward her with a stare.

"It is hard to smoke in blowing rain," I tell her.

"Don't mind my fucking business."

I shunt a Camel above the rim of the hard box toward her. She dips her head and takes it with her mouth.

With a look she asks me for a light. I light mine first and hold the match toward her. She does not move. The flame begins to creep toward my fingers. This has now become a test of wills. She is trying to unsettle me. She wants to show me how bad she can be. The truth is that I do not need convincing. She has craft. She has wiles. She has played the saint for years, and she is a devil.

I can smell my burning flesh. I do not wince. I raise the fire to her face. She lights it with a birdish dip and sucks the Camel deeply.

I watch her cheeks collapse then flare. When she eases back I see the frailness of her throat. Her eyelids flicker as she blows the smoke. I suck my burning finger.

"So tell me," she says as our smoke begins to mingle. "What did my husband say?"

"That he isn't having an affair."

"Do you believe him?"

"Yes," I lie.

"Why?"

"He's not the type."

"There is no type, Carey. Like apples, people fall."

"I know about falling. I have fallen many times."

"Many people have fallen, Carey. You would think that those who fall would learn."

"You're upset, so you are entitled."

"Entitled to what?"

"To be the way you are being."

"Which is what?"

"A bitch."

"You haven't seen a bitch yet, Carey. You will see a bitch when I divorce your friend."

"Divorce him for what?"

"I don't know. I will try to find a reason. I can't live like this anymore."

"Like how?"

"He never has time to take care of us. He is always on the road. My husband doesn't love me anymore. He just doesn't know how to say it."

"That's not true."

"How does he show it, Carey?"

"I am not always here."

"So just fucking listen to what I tell you then. Listen to me and learn."

"Nazia, I have to be fair. I cannot take sides. Plus you shouldn't be here right now. You should be working things out with him."

"Like a good woman." She jabs with her hand. "You didn't say anything when I told you that he pushed me."

"Were you standing in his way?" I prod. "Did you push him first?"

"Yes. I pushed him first. I slapped him, too. But that is not the point. The point is that he's driven me to this."

"What if he comes in here and . . . I don't know. He already cussed me out for entertaining you at night. I need to pack and leave. You need to work this out with your husband. Fuck it. Fuck the two of you. Good night."

I toss the cigarette through the window. She tosses hers as well. I sit on the bed with my face in my hands. I hear her close the window. There is a sniffle, then a cough, then the shuffling of the canvas off her shoulders.

What did Kwabena tell her? What would I do if he should come right now? Would it be ugly?

When I look again she is standing by the sofa. There is a shirt over her sari. It is green. There are plastic bangles on her wrists.

"You cannot leave right now," she says. She walks away to close the other windows. "It makes no sense. There is too much rain."

With the windows closed the smell of the room asserts itself, a smell of mud and smoke and perspiration.

I want her to leave, but she sits there with her elbows on her knees. Leaning forward in lament, she reaches with her palms behind her neck. Water dribbles from her hair against the table.

"Nazia," I say. "What is going on?"

She does not look at me. She motions me to sit with her.

In the matching chair across from her I catch her scent. She smells of salt and rain.

I tell her to dry her hair. She sweeps it backward, looks up and palms her face, reappearing slickly through her fingers like a newly surfaced seal.

"The chair is getting soaked."

"It's mine," she says. "I can do what I want."

"Okay, Nazia. Fuck you."

I kick the table and it stops just short of bumping her. This is not like me.

"Carey, don't do that!"

"Why? Are you afraid of me? Do you think that I'm a nut? Do you think that I will cut your throat and shoot your man and rape your little children?"

I am shouting and I want to stop myself but I can't. Am I crazy? Is this what madness feels like? Wanting to stop but not stopping?

"Carey, don't do that!"

She curls up on the sofa and begins to cry.

"Why not? It's the truth."

"Who told you that? Who told you that?"

"Your husband, Nazia. Your husband." I cannot stop myself. "He told me how you woke up in the night and told him that you didn't like the way that I was keeping to myself because you found it frightening. Then you told him that I need to see a shrink. So you pressured him to do your dirty work. If you wanted me to go *you* should have asked me to go. Why put the man in that position? You are so full of fucking shit. You said that you were frightened I would harm you or the children." She bites a cushion now. "Do you think that I would really fucking hurt you, Nazia? Is that where your fucking head resides? Do you think that I would hurt those kids? How could you do that to your husband? Knowing what he is going through? How could you pressure him that way? The poor man couldn't do it, so he tries to get away by saying that he's going down to Greelyville—just to get away from doing what you are pressuring him to do. And then you have the gall to come and tell me that you think that he is fucking someone else?"

"I didn't say these things. How could you believe that? Why would anyone say that?"

"Just to give you practice being hysterical."

"Ohhhhhhhhhh . . ."

"Leave," I command her. "Get out of here. Just go."

"I didn't say those things," she whispers through the beating of the rain. "My husband lied to you. He hates you, Carey. He envies you. That is not the way the conversation went." She wipes her face against her sleeve. "I woke up in the middle of the night, and I asked him how come he wasn't spending time with you. He told me you were writing. I told him that I thought that you were really troubled, that what you really needed now was love from us, your closest friends. You were withdrawing from everyone. From me. From him. The kids. You weren't even doing soccer anymore. Whatever I said he just answered, 'He is writing. He's all right.' Everything I said he kept repeating that until I said that maybe you were deeply depressed and that I was really worried. Then he said I was a sucker. I asked him what he meant. He asked me how much mileage did I think that you deserved from this suicide thing. He said you use that as a ploy, as an easy way to get over. And when I said this wasn't so he said I was naïve. And then he went on his usual thing."

"What usual thing is that?"

Her nostrils flatten as she draws a breath.

"That you are a fraud with a bit of talent. That you are a hustler. That you don't believe in anything. That you are nothing but a charmer."

I know another liar when I see one. Nazia is telling the truth.

"He hates you, Carey. He envies you. He wants everything that you have. He hates it that you were on TV. He hates it that you don't live in your parents' house. He hates it that you don't have children to distract you. He hates you for not coming when you said you would. He wanted that exposure in the *Sunday Times* like you will never know. He feels fucked over. He feels so used. He hates you, Carey. He hates you really badly. He hates you but he loves you. Carey, he loves you, man. And that is why this whole thing is so hard for him. He wants you to go, but he doesn't know how to do it. So he blamed it on me. He lied to you. I don't hate you, Carey. I love you."

I am stunned into silence. She looks for something to dry her hair, grabs the bundled tank with which I wiped myself and slowly wipes her face. I want to stop her but I cannot speak. Plus, nothing matters anymore.

Kwabena hates me. Yes, he loves me but he also hates me. He lied to me and he lied to his wife. He made me hate his wife. He made me hate his wife. He made me hate his fucking wife, who loves me.

I cannot look at her. I cannot look at her. Not with the rain outside and the anger that I feel toward her husband.

I close my eyes to shut her out and find behind my lids, flickering on pause, the fantasy that had drawn me in before her arrival. My body is demanding action. I need to be alone.

"I cannot leave you this way," she says as I show her to the door. "Let's at least be decent."

In an awkward sense of normalcy we make our final supper: coffee, crackers, and sweaty cheese. This is not reconciliation. We are simply tired, tired of betrayals, tired of lies, tired of being suspicious.

"So, Carey, what are you going to do when you return?" she asks, facing me over her mug.

"Oh, I have a lot of things to do. And you?"

"Study. The kids. That is my life."

"You have given up a lot."

"You do stupid things for love."

"And when will you be done with school?"

"It all depends on Kwabena. He's got all that he needs . . . a stupid wife, lovely kids, a great house in which to live, a teaching job with tenure—and a mistress on the side. That's all that really counts."

I block him out. He does not exist for me right now. If I think of him, he will make me angry again. And I want to be calm right now.

So he hates me? He hates me? He hates me? The fucking bastard hates me. How the fuck did he get a wife like this?

"Do you know what you're going to study?"

"Considering what I've gotten myself into. I'm clearly stupid. You can't picture me in college, can you, Mr. Cambridge?"

"I didn't mean it like that. In any case I flunked out."

"Well, how do you see me?" she challenges.

"As Nazia. Kwabena's wife—"

"See. That is all you can see. There is so much more to me."

"I wasn't finished."

"I know," she says. She blows across the mug to cool it and her breath seeps into my mouth. It is an awkward moment. She begins to apologize, then shakes her head and laughs.

"And the woman in the poems?" she begins again. "How does she fit in?"

"Our situation is extremely complicated."

"Do you love her?"

"I do."

"Does she know it?"

"Perhaps."

"What is so complicated though?"

I take a sip and answer as I lean back in the chair. "A lot of things. We don't live in the same place. We are not from the same place. Then there is a problem with Kwabena."

I should not have said that. The mood has changed. She is agitated now. She stands and starts to smooth her hair and clothes.

"I have to go," she says weakly.

And as I walk her to the door she stops and turns around.

"Carey, how long have you been in love with me?"

She kisses first. Her tongue is soft. If I didn't know better I would say experienced.

As I pull away I feel a switch being pushed inside me, thrusting me to action. I resist.

"What was that?" I ask.

My voice is not as hard as I expected.

"Your reward," she replies. "Your reward for being my friend all these years, for saving me from myself. I have always been so weak for you. And you have always known this. But you never took advantage."

"I am not in love with you, Nazia. And I didn't know you were in love with me. Go now before this conversation gets us into trouble."

She wipes her mouth with the back of her hand.

"I can see through your pants that you are hard," she says as she offers her hand. "What does that mean?"

"It has nothing to do with you."

"Of course it does. It has everything to do with me."

"I don't love you, Nazia," I emphasize. "And you are not in love with me. You are angry with your husband."

"And so are you. Don't think of love right now. Don't think of who loves who or why. Think of hate. Only hate. Think of hate and fuck me. Fucking me would be the best revenge."

She is small beneath the coat. Slender but soft, and she quails at my touch as if her flesh were made of petals and my hands were tongues of flame.

"He hardly fucks me anymore," she says. She leads me to the bed. She kneels there with her back toward the wall, reaching round behind her for the knot that holds the sari.

In a black brassiere and panties made of cotton she reclines against the ivory sheets, her face dissolved into the shadows.

"I can't," I say. "There are no condoms."

"So lick me then."

Her voice is dreamy. Her words are interspersed with moans and purrs. "I have only made love to one man in my life. I have never felt the way I know I ought to feel."

"Which is how?"

"Rejuvenated. Born again. I want to feel the rush and fear of passing through a tiny space and spurting through the universe."

I reach for her across the sheets and pull her down toward me.

From the foot of the bed I watch her, her nutty brownness, her girlish breasts, her simple bra, the trace of ribs beneath the skin.

Her hips are like an apple sliced in two.

She arches as I stroke her side, begins to move like she is swimming underwater, pulling up her knees and stretching them slowly, reaching back behind her with her arms.

"I have wanted you for years," she moans. This bothers me. "There is a way in which you look at me sometimes. Like the first morning when you came and you found me in the kitchen at the table with my books. God, I just wanted you to hold me and say, 'Baby, I miss you.' I came back that morning just to see you. I just had to see you again. Sure, Tano had left something behind. But I just wanted to see you."

Don't mention the children, I want to say. If I think of them I cannot do this.

I begin to feel a change of heart. I cannot do this anymore.

Then she hooks a finger in her panties and draws them to the side and I glimpse a glistening flower made of folded tongues. She lets the fabric snap against her skin, trapping wispy hairs.

"He never gets me wet like this."

"Nazia."

"So when he tells me lies I get so fucking angry. I get so fucking angry, Carey. I hate him when he hates you. I hate him when he hates you. I hate him when he hates you. I hate him."

I hate him, too. I hate him, too. I fucking hate him, too.

I reach between my legs and think of Frances, pulling Nazia's flavor through the fabric like the taste of cream through cupcake paper.

Afterward, we lay together in the little bed, clinging to each other like survivors on a raft.

"What happens next?" she whispers. I don't know what to say. She answers for the both of us. "In many ways the choices have been made."

She continues talking, but I cannot hear. My mind is far away, over the Atlantic, looking down at pumice-colored waves.

Where is my woman? What is she doing? Is she well? Is she happy? Does she miss me?

As Nazia starts to coax me with her hand I get the sudden rush of falling.

Where is she? Where is she? Where am I? Where? Not here. Not here in this room with my brother's wife. Nazia is right. The choices have been made. The choices have been made. I am falling. I am falling. Falling into water.

"You are coming," Nazia whispers. "You are coming."

I have to leave this place. I have to go and find where the palm trees sing hosanna in the harmattan wind.

CHAPTER TWENTY-SIX

Viewed at night from the gaps between the clouds, Ghana is a land of oceanic darkness. Along the coast there is an archipelago of lights: Axim, Sekondi, Elmina, Cape Coast, Winneba, towns as subtle as bars of sand, then the phosphorescent mass of Accra.

Go north across this line of lights and there is darkness once again—as if the sea has drowned the country, exterminating everything, with few survivors. Kumasi and Tamale show like reefs in shallow water.

In daylight Ghana shows itself to be a land of substance, a nation of 17 million people chorusing in sixty different languages, a rectangle as large as Britain.

From the coastline, moving with the country's length, scrub and plains give way to clotted forests. From the forest belt the land ascends into a low plateau of woodland and savanna.

Here in the north, twelve hours by car from the coast, half an hour to the border with Burkina Faso, the seasons move in fluid cycles.

From May to September it rains. In October desert dryness trails the harmattan, a wind that wears a snapping, flapping coat

of dust that lines your softest tissues with a burlap roughness—
your itching nose, your gasping mouth, your watery eyes. In
the harmattan season the sky is screened with a calico haze that
renders birds and clouds as apparitions.

Now it is March, the hot season, and the air is limp and un-
moving, a hundred and ten degrees, damp as a body wracked
with fever.

Relief will come in May; then, the flamboyant trees will
bloom. Their wide branches will erupt with red and orange
blossoms; their flat, black pods will stand out keenly in relief
against the sere landscape like newly forged machetes; the dust
will be dissolved by rain; the haze will unravel and re-form itself
as clouds of rolling cotton; dry ravines will moil with streams;
dirt roads will cream with mud; and farmers will leave their village walls and spread out in their fields, planting groundnuts,
cotton, okra, rice, and millet—crops that can be reaped within
the confines of a four-month growing season.

From my home among a grove of baobab trees that crown
the only hill for miles, I stand and watch the cycles that define
this harsh environment. From here the view is panoramic. The
dirt is red and rocky. The trees are few and meager. And the
grass is wheat-brown in this place whose flatness calls to mind a
prairie.

The *kraals* are small, the houses made of mud and roofed
with thatch. The nearest town is thirty miles away.

Toward the west, sheared from view by the horizon, is a
sacred pond. Sometimes in the mornings, if no one comes to see
me, I will twitch my robe about myself and travel there,
descending from my mountain.

Like the trees, which have been harvested for firewood for
centuries, most of the animals are gone. Sometimes along the
way there is a herd of antelopes, sometimes a pack of jackals or
hyenas.

Walking reminds me of the man I used to be before I made my transition.

Yes, my friend. I have died.

The sacred pond is a favorite watering hole of Hora spirits. We go there to meet and talk and drink, pickling ourselves with *pito*, a hearty millet beer, which we sip from gourds as we lament our prospects like day laborers.

We have never been many. Since my transition I have come to learn that we did not originate in Ghana, but in southeastern Sudan, close to Ethiopia, and were led here four thousand years ago by a mad prophet who thought that he had found the way to China. Of the ten thousand ancestors who began the journey, only eight hundred survived, and from that remnant we became again as much as fifteen thousand. Now we are less than five hundred.

"Karamoko, the wanderer who always returns."

This is how they always greet me. My response is usually the same. I wave them off like flies and sit by myself and brood.

There is nothing spiritual about us. We are as cantankerous as human beings. We curse. We fight. We tell lies, and we make alliances against one another, all in the name of power. When we are bored or in need of objects that will appease the gods we harass human beings, knowing that they will come to us for help. Yes, we have our little racket. We are badly out of tune. On special days we tune ourselves to the frequency of *iz*, the spirit force. But this is an empty ritual, like humans gracing meals.

The ritual that means the most to us is complaining. At the sacred pond the conversation is unchanging: How do we get more people to believe?

Most Ghanaians are Christian. Here in the north there are

many Muslims, but Christianity is winning more converts every day. The ritual of complaint is rambunctious but comforting, for it gives us a reason to exist.

The explanations for the growth of Christianity are always the same: A fiberoptic cable is an intravenous feeder streaming Western poison ... foreign televangelists buy allegiance with free food ... the American pop stars, especially the black ones, always thank the white God when they get their awards, so our people think that the white God will bring them fame and money. . . .

The solutions are always the same as well: The Rastafarians have reggae and the *orishas* in Brazil have the samba, so we need to get ourselves some sexy music ... the Yoruba have done well with the black people in America; we should concentrate on them for they are always looking for something different ... we should go and speak with Onyame, the chief god of the Ashanti and tell him that we are sorry that our stupid Karamoko interfered with the marriage of Feranje to the Asantahene and see if he will forgive us and make us honorary Ashanti spirits, because this Hora thing is not working out.

When the other speakers are exhausted, Shiro, the half-man half-god who appears to his believers as a thin albino, will give his speech. Shiro's insteps end in snarling crocodiles. At the pond he likes to rest his feet against the carcass of a warthog or a wildebeest and listen to the feeding of his frenzied toes.

"I have been saying for years. There is only one way out. We should murder all the Hora people left alive. If we didn't have believers there would be nothing to lament. We could have the idle life of angels."

So this is what my days are like. In the evenings I return to my mountain to receive devotion from the only person who believes in me.

Kana does not always come. She is a slender poet ... young, with matted hair and bloodshot eyes. Through the dirt and sores her beauty is insistent like the rhythm on a damaged forty-five. Her face is heart-shaped; her cheekbones show like boomerangs below her desert-colored skin. When her eyes are clear you see their glow. With flesh, her pelvic bones, which hold her skin slackly, would mount a voluptuous roundness.

I met her when I first arrived. I was circling the air above Accra searching for my love when I noticed a commotion in Makola Market.

Accra is a sprawling city of bungalows and low-rise concrete buildings, most of which are white or cream. It is a city by the sea, but it is not a major port, so it is not a city that reverberates with new ideas. There are few tourists here.

Unlike the vehicles that ply them, the roads are good and new. There are no cafés. When Ghanaians dine outside they gather around a woman at a table heaped with rice and bowls of sauce.

I was not yet good at flight. The ways of the spirit world are contrary. There are no guides. You are left to discover your capacities on your own. I discovered that I could fly accidentally. Forgetting for a moment that I had made my transition, I leapt out of the way of a truck and took to the sky. But then I had to learn through trial and error that my hands control climbing and diving, that my shoulder blades control a turn, that braking is a matter of controlling the breath, but acceleration is controlled by blinking the eyes.

I had not yet discovered the switch for telescopic vision, so I was hovering about thirty feet above Kojo Thompson Road, peering into faces, looking at shapes, learning to identify people by their tribes, able to understand only those who spoke English and Hora, for I could not locate the filter that would allow me to understand other languages. The street was thick with taxis and minibuses, which I had just learned were called *tro-tros*. The sidewalk was clotted with hawkers—hawkers selling mounds of used American shoes and clothes, hawkers selling fluttering hankies pinned along the ribs of open parasols, hawkers selling Embassy and Diplomat cigarettes and Star beer from cardboard boxes slung around their necks, and in between the hawkers shoe shine boys hustling in the dust.

Hovering is achieved by a complicated set of coordinated considerations, much like treading water; so, being an unsupervised apprentice, I descended to earth, assumed human form and began to walk among the people.

Assuming human form is always risky. We become as vulnerable as seals on land. In human form we are old and lame. After more than an hour it is hard for us to breathe. The witches are aware of this, and they are always ready with their spells. To reassume our spirit form we have to find a quiet place and chant a special prayer. This is when we are most at risk, because the prayer requires deep concentration. Yes, this is when the witches pounce and stun us with a dash of fresh blood drawn from the heart of a newborn and bind our wrists and ankles with living snakes. Then we become their servants—a fate considered worse than death.

So I was hobbling along Kojo Thompson Road, dressed in Western clothes like the people around me to avert all suspicion, learning the place, noticing things, when I saw Kana.

I had just crossed over Kinbu Road, moving with the slope in the direction of the sea, when I saw ahead of me a big commotion. Makola Market is more than a place to trade. Over the years it has grown beyond its walls to become a shanty village in the middle of the central business district. It ignores the order carved into the landscape by British men. It is run and largely patronized by African women.

When I approached the crowd I saw a mob encircling Kana, who had been accused of cooking and consuming a missing child. She was innocent, I could tell, an easy choice for blame. I had seen her before, an eccentric who slept naked on an anthill near Legon.

Kana had amassed through theft and scavenging an eight-foot mound of shoes. From listening to the crowd I learned that she had spent the last three weeks declaring in rhyming couplets that Shiro had commanded her to set her mound of shoes on fire and feed the ashes to the crocodile that lived in her vagina.

There was something in her spirit that reminded me of Frances—and at the risk of being captured by a witch I transformed again into a spirit, snatched her from the angry mob, and soared into the sky.

Now Kana lives at the foot of my mountain in a hut beneath a tree.

The spirits at the sacred pond avoid her. She is bad for their image. She is bad for mine as well. And she understands this. If a person from a nearby village comes to see me she will stay inside her hut.

This evening Kana brings an offering of *fufu* and *kontomreh*. Most times she brings me fruit. She keeps her delicate mice and roasted dung at home.

Kana likes to talk to me about America.

In this life she was born in Detroit. When she was a child she wanted to be a poet. She published her first book at twenty-one. The book was reviewed in the *New York Times*. She began to feel assured of her future. Then things began to change.

As she tells it, one night as she wrote, the words began to come in another language. At first she resisted it, translated it in her head. Three months later she began to see another set of words between the lines. Six months later she developed the capacity to read these words. When she started writing papers in this language she was encouraged to see a doctor.

Sometimes as we eat she will mention the asylum—but she never lingers there. Neither will she dwell on her escape. Whenever I ask her how she came to Ghana, her answer is the same: "I swam."

Sometimes she will speak of the child that she carried.

Sometimes she will speak of the men that she loved. Sometimes she will speak of the men who stone her when she hides outside a village wall to scavenge food that has been left for dogs.

"Stoning is their way of showing fear," she always says. Her voice is finely modulated. It is clear that she was born into a family of means. "I am simply too much woman for those losers. It takes a lot of man to satisfy a woman with a hungry crocodile between her legs."

Sometimes she will cry and tell me that she wants to go home to Michigan, that she would love to remember, if only for a minute, the route she took across the Atlantic.

As we eat this evening, she points a broken finger to a gash above her knee. I ask her how she got it.

"In Navorongo," she says, avoiding my eyes.

"And how did you get there?" I prod.

"I walked," she says weakly.

"You walked thirty miles in the heat?" I challenge.

"Yes. Yes. To read a poem in the market."

In five years I will have the power to choke her with invisible vines. Now all I have is words.

"You are not telling the truth," I declare.

She sighs and then confesses.

"I went to the cathedral. I wanted to see it before—"

In my head I see the mud cathedral. Its beauty is exquisite.

Kana knows that she is about to die. Catholic in her last in-carnation, she went to the cathedral because she felt compelled to talk to Christ.

I am offended. But I understand. But where was Jesus when the mob encircled her? I want to ask this, but I don't. Like many African spirits, I have a grudging admiration for the Lord.

In the confusing days that followed my return I lost my way in flight and landed in Oyo, Nigeria. I was fortunate enough to have an audience with Legba, the trickster god of the Yoruba.

"Baba," I asked, "what happened to you and Shango and Ogun in the middle passage? Where were our great spirits?"

Legba looked over his shoulder and whispered: "I can only speak for myself. But here it is I am *the* trickster god of Nigeria, the greatest trickster nation that this world has ever seen and this Christ man comes along and pulls off history's greatest hustle. That resurrection thing is the kind of act that no one wants to follow. Now a good trickster can bring off a crucifixion. But coming back is another thing. Christ frightened me. It is as simple as that. The man had too much skill. I will take him on at home before a partisan crowd. Away is a different sort of thing. It is rough out there on the road. What if we had gone across the sea to challenge him and lost? Our people would be left completely in despair. We stayed away to give you hope."

For the first three months of my return I was hopeless. Death did not arrive with instructions. The transition was instantaneous. There were no paths. There were no shafts of light.

Nazia was curled against me in the bed. The rain was coming hard. At first we did not hear Kwabena's knock. When we did we did not move.

"Go through the window," Nazia urged me.

"There is no point in doing that."

"Yes. He has a gun."

He had surprised me once again. He pushed the door. His shadow filled the space. One arm seemed longer than the next.

"Kwabena," I called out. "Please put it down."

He placed the muzzle in his mouth and shuffled to the bed, emerging from the darkness to the light like a print on photographic paper. Nazia gasped when she saw him. She clung to me. As I held her close I felt her muscles slacken when she fainted from the fright.

"Kwabena. Put it down," I said again.

He answered with the muzzle in his mouth.

"What is there to live for?"

There was a flash of lightning.

"What do you mean? The children. The children. Forget me and you and Nazia. The children."

"The children?" He pressed the gun against his lower lip and stretched his jaw. "The children? The children? They are already gone."

"What do you mean? You killed them?"

He nodded. I was not sure if I believed him. I had not heard the shots. But then I did not think that this could happen. I did not know he had a gun.

The gun was small. Perhaps a twenty-two. In the driving rain, perhaps, I had missed the sound. But what if he was lying?

"You would never kill your children," I bluffed. "You would never kill those kids."

I eased his wife away from me and sat up in the bed. "Let's talk about this thing," I said. "Let's talk about this thing. Forget me and you and Nazia and Frances and this whole fucking mess. Let us make this all about the children. You love those children. Those children love you. Give the gun to me. They cannot grow up without you. You have to live for them. You cannot go out like this. Kwabena, where is God in all of this? You are a child of God, man." I began to walk toward him. He backed away toward the door. "If you do this, what is going to happen to your soul? What is going to happen to your soul, Kwabena?" He did not answer. "Where are the children? Where are the children?"

He stopped, removed the gun from his mouth and answered: "How could you do this to me?"

Over my shoulder Nazia stirred. I turned to look at her. She was still disoriented.

"Kwabena," she began, "what are you doing here?"

His face was blank. He leaned his head to the left and peered at her, didn't seem to find what he was looking for and looked at her directly.

"What am I doing here?" he asked coolly. "I'm trying to communicate with you. I'm trying to let you know how I feel. I feel as if I am the world's most gigantic failure. After everything I told you about the way he makes me feel you went ahead and slept with him."

"We didn't have sex," I interjected.

"So what did you do?"

He pointed the gun at her head. The question wasn't mine.

"I touched him with my hands," she confessed, "and he put his mouth on me."

"Did you fuck him?"

"Kwabena—"

He swung the gun at me.

"Kwabena," I said again. "You have the gun so you have the power. I am asking permission to speak with you."

"Did you ask permission to fuck my wife?"

"No. But I did not have sex with her. We did inappropriate things. But not the things that you have in your mind."

"Do you know what I have in my mind?"

"Of course I don't."

"I have it in my mind for you to ask me permission to fuck her. Say after me, 'Kwabena, may I fuck your wife?' "

"Kwabena . . . may I fuck your wife?"

"Yes, Carey, you may. Now go ahead and fuck her."

"No, I can't."

"Yes, you can."

"Let's fucking talk this out."

"Don't talk to me like that, Carey. How could you humiliate me this way?"

"Kwa—"

"So are you going to fuck her?"

"No."

He began to laugh.

"Do you see how arrogant you are? I am holding a gun to you, and you think you have the right to tell me no. Well, Mr. Superstar, I know that you are accustomed to having choices." He began to undo his fly. "Fuck my wife or suck my dick."

I closed my eyes. "Just go ahead," I said, "and fucking kill me."

"Of course you wouldn't suck my dick. You want to fuck my wife. But you're too embarrassed to do it in front of my face. But the minute I turn my back, I know, you will flip her over."

"You are delusional, Kwabena. Put away the gun."

He began to gesture with his other hand.

"Now why would a man like me be delusional? I can't get a fucking play produced. I lost my fucking house. My best friend has taken both the first woman I ever loved and the last woman I will ever love away from me. I have a fucking right."

"Put away the gun."

"I'm still using it."

"Put away the fucking gun and stop this madness now."

"Do you know that I came here right behind her? Do you know that I was listening the whole time?"

When he said this shame overpowered anger and I closed my eyes again.

"Just shoot me," I told him. "Get it over with. I want to die."

The sound of the bullet flung me back into the sheets.

No, Kwabena did not shoot me. Kwabena shot his wife. And as I turned to help there was another sound, an echo on the edge of consciousness ... an echo then a sigh, a sigh then a grunt, a grunt that introduced a thick dull thump as a body hit a floor ... a thump then a crack ... the crack of a skull on a floor, a crack and then the smack of wet flesh.

The blood streamed from a neat hole in her temple. Nazia was dead.

On the floor, Kwabena thrashed about. His face was tight, but surprisingly unruffled, as if he were reacting to nothing more serious than a stench.

"Jesus Christ, Kwabena. Kwabena, Jesus Christ."

His eyes were turning out of focus. He coughed and tried to speak. I expected blood but there was none.

I knelt and cradled him. When I reached behind his head my fingers were quicksanded in a muck of blood and brain and shattered bone.

"Kwabena. Kwabena. Look at what you have done. Where are the children?"

"The children?" His cheeks began to slacken with a smile. "God will take care of them. Carey, I will see you in hell."

I grabbed the gun and ran out in the rain. Dumbly, as if I thought that he would recover and give pursuit.

The children were unharmed. He had been bluffing. I called the police. I walked outside and stood in the rain. The woman that I slept with on my final night on earth was dead and I had killed her. She was my neighbor's wife.

I did not hear the gun. I felt the hole. I felt my body deflating. I felt the rush as my spirit escaped and caught a current that carried it home. But I did not hear the gun. My final memory from that incarnation was the coldness of the steel against my temple.

I arrived here expecting to see Frances Carey. But she had already moved on.

When she landed in Accra she went to see the *futah*, the man with whom she had the disagreement. He told her that if she did not pay the money he would send Shiro to take her life. She had gone to see him even though she had undergone a change. The day before she saw him, she had returned to the church where she had been christened as a child and asked the priest to wash her once again in the blood of Christ, not because she wanted to, but because the man she loved had asked.

Yes, she intended to return to me.

But when she went to see the *futah*, he tried to hold her hostage and she fought him and escaped. He could have sent a henchman but instead he sent Shiro. In the morning Frances Carey was discovered bloodied on a beach outside Accra. According to the papers she was robbed.

I have never raised the issue with Shiro. I understand that one day, as a spirit, I too will be called upon to do horrific things. That is life on earth.

Kana will make her transition in the morning. I know this because I am a spirit. Then I will lose touch with her because spirits cannot go to after worlds where they have not been invited.

I cannot see my father. I cannot see Frances. I cannot see my children.

As Kana walks away I accept the burden of the truth. And I await the knowledge of how and when I will make the transition to another cycle of human life.

Will I meet Frances again? Now that she has gone to heaven will she even want me? If Christianity is right then it means that I will go to hell. There is a part of me that wants this. I need to speak with Kwabena. I need to speak to Nazia. I need to speak with my father.

You, who have read the story of my life, what have you learned from my mistakes? Who do you love? What do you believe? What do you think lies behind the curtain of this life? Do you even know who you are? Or what you are?

You are merely a spirit in the middle of having a human experience. You have lived before and you will live again.

What will happen to me? I do not know. I want to see my woman again so I will put my trust in God. I will have to find a way to get to heaven. Yes, I am a traitor. Yes, I live in the world of African spirits but I am putting my destiny in the hand of the white man's God. Yes, Jesus saves.

Why? Do I think he is greater? That is not the point. I simply want to be with my woman. And if this is what it will take then I will surrender. But will he take me? I do not know.

All is lost. All is lost. Jesus Christ has won.

● ACKNOWLEDGMENTS

The first word of this book was written in 1995. In the interven-
ing years friends with differing abilities volunteered their time
to help to make it better. No one made their contribution with
the end of seeing their name in print, so I will spare them the in-
dignity of roll-call listings and honor them with a moment of
silence.

But a writer must thank his agent and his editor. Marie Brown
and Anita Diggs, you offered consistent wise counsel.

A father must thank his children. Addis and Makonnen, you
consistently offered the kind of compelling distraction that puts
all things in perspective.

A husband must thank his wife. Bridgitte, living with me has
never been easy. I could never be married to me!

A colleague must thank his comrades. Ben Bailey and all the
members of the creative team that built Eziba, you illuminated
and transformed me with your passion. More fire!

An author must thank the writers whose work inspired him
as he wrote. Pauline Melville, I learned a lot from reading *The
Ventriloqist's Tale*. Ronan Bennett, *The Catastrophist* doubled
my courage to write a novel in the first person, present tense.

A patriot must thank his country. Jamaica, you are the most beautiful country in the world. Jamaicans, you are the most beautiful people. One love.

And a survivor must thank the ones who died. The price for my freedom was paid in blood. Thanks be to God.